THE SHERIFF OF WHISKEY CITY

Book One
in
The Whiskey City
Series

THE SHERIFF OF WHISKEY CITY

Book One
in
The Whiskey City
Series

•

ROBIN GIBSON

WESTERN
GIBSON
c.1

AVALON BOOKS
THOMAS BOUREGY AND COMPANY, INC.
401 LAFAYETTE STREET
NEW YORK, NEW YORK 10003

PRINTED IN THE UNITED STATES OF AMERICA
ON ACID-FREE PAPER
BY HADDON CRAFTSMEN, SCRANTON, PENNSYLVANIA

To my sister, Mona

Chapter One

I reckon it all started peaceful enough.

I was just sitting out front of the jail, trying to keep my whole body in the shade, which ain't easy for a man my size. No matter how I twisted and turned, I couldn't quite fit in that patch of shade. Yawning, I settled for having my boots sticking out in the sun. Right then, I don't reckon I had a clue as to what was in store for Whiskey City. Like a fool, I figured I had the world by the tail.

Now, despite its colorful name, Whiskey City ain't a very exciting town. Which suits me just fine, seeing's how I'm the new sheriff. Now, don't go gettin' me wrong, I ain't claiming that I'm a lawman by trade. I was a rancher for a while, till my cows up and died. Then I tried my hand at farming, but nothing I planted ever came up.

It's likely that I woulda starved to death, but the folks of Whiskey City took pity on me, giving me the sheriff's job after Vance Sellers quit. The reason Vance gave for quitting was that he was bored

1

with the job. The gossip around town held a different opinion. Seems like Vance had been trying to spark one of old man Wiesmulluer's daughters, and the old man found out.

Wiesmulluer had two of the prettiest daughters you ever did see. Trouble was, that old man was meaner than a longhorn bull with a case of the piles. Not only that, he was tougher than a hotel steak, so most folks figured Vance scooted out of town before he got his backside branded with the imprint of the old man's boot. Not that anyone faulted Vance for skedaddling. No, sir, not a soul in Whiskey City dared cross Wiesmulluer . . . well, nobody except Louis Claude.

Local legend has it that Whiskey City came to be because Wiesmulluer got into a scrap with the little Frenchman, Claude. The way I heard it, both men were part of a wagon train heading west. One night, the wagons camped on the very spot where Whiskey City now stands. The next morning, when the wagons were fixing to roll out, Wiesmulluer and Claude commenced to jawing about who's wagon should be first in line. I don't reckon the jawing lasted long, not knowing those two.

Now, the first time I heard about the fight, the story was they battled for just over an hour. The last time I heard the story, the fight lasted three hours. Since I wasn't there, you can take your pick which version to believe. Either way, by the time they got all the fussin' and fightin' out of their systems, neither man was in any shape to travel, and the rest of the folks were tuckered out from cheering, so the whole wagon train stayed. Several years later, most of them folks were still here.

Every so often, Wiesmulluer and Claude will meet in town and have a sort of reenactment of the founding of Whiskey City. I have seen several of them battles, and believe me, they are real humdingers. You wouldn't think they would be thataway, not sizing the two of them up. Wiesmulluer stands a raw-boned six feet, maybe even a bit more. You'd think he could whip the world. He has a craggy face, with a skinny hawk nose and long white eyebrows that look like horns on a steer. All in all, his face looks like the wrath of God.

Claude on the other hand is a smooth-faced little feller. He looks kinda meek, but just like Wiesmulluer, Claude has the devil's own temper. And while Wiesmulluer is the bigger man, Claude is quicker. Plus, Claude knows some kind of fancy kick fighting. Last time the two fought, Claude kicked Wiesmulluer in the face, breaking that hawk nose.

In the salon, hanging behind the bar, is a board with both of their names carved in it. Under each name is a bunch of marks, each mark for a fight won by that man. So far the score reads six fights for Wiesmulluer and five for Claude. Under the board sets a gallon glass jar crammed full of money, where folks have already placed their bets for the next fight.

But other than that, nothing much ever happens in Whiskey City. That is, until Bobby Stamper rode into town.

Like I said, it started peaceful enough. He rode up the street bold as brass, tipping his hat at Iris Winkler, who was hanging out her wash. I stood up, giving him a right stern look as I returned his wave with a curt nod of my head. Now, at the time, I had no idea who this smiling stranger was, but I wanted to let him know that the sheriff of Whiskey

City was on the job and wasn't about to stand for any funny business.

"Howdy, Sheriff," the stranger called, giving me another wave as he dismounted in front of the saloon.

No trouble there, I decided, settling back into my chair. Forgetting about him, I tipped backed my chair and closed my eyes. I'd just gotten good and comfortable when somebody went to screeching like a cat with her tail caught in the gate. Opening one eye, I saw that Gid Stevens' dog had got into Mrs. Winkler's laundry, pulling some of her bloomers off the line. That dog was making his getaway with that old woman in hot pursuit.

Now, Mrs. Iris Winkler might seem to be a kindly widow, but believe me, it didn't appear that-away when she took off after that mutt. You shoulda heard the cussing she gave that dog, all the while chasing the poor critter with a shovel, flogging him in the backside. She got in a couple of good licks before the shovel handle snapped off in her hands.

As that dog ran off yelping, Mrs. Winkler stalked over to where I sat. "You're the sheriff, and I want you to do something about that dog," she said, shaking the splintered end of that shovel handle in my face.

I leaned back, half-scared she was gonna gouge out one of my eyes, the way she was waving the handle around. "Yes, ma'am, I'll speak to Gid," I promised.

Mrs. Winkler snorted, whipping that shovel handle by my nose. "That won't do any good. If Gid Stevens wanted to do something about that mutt, he already would have done it. Lord knows he never spends any time in that store of his."

That was true enough. Gid Stevens had a peculiar way of running a business: he just opened the door and left. Come to think of it, I don't even recall if the place had a door. I never seen it shut. Gid didn't have time to stay in the store, not when there was a saloon close by with cold beer and someone to shoot the bull with or rope into a game of dominoes. Folks just went inside and got what they needed and wrote it down. Then, whenever Gid needed money, he would go around and collect, usually mooching a meal in the process.

"Are you listening to me?" Mrs. Winkler asked, and before I knew it, the old bat cracked me on the shin with that shovel handle.

Yelping, I grabbed my injured shin, dancing around on one foot. To tell the truth, I'd been daydreaming and hadn't been listening to her blabbering.

"Somebody better do something about that dog, or I will!" Iris growled.

As Mrs. Winkler marched off, I kicked back and settled into my chair, reminding myself to watch Gid's dog the next time she washed clothes.

I sat there, reflecting that this was the good life. I wondered why I hadn't taken up sheriffing a long time ago. I mean, I spent three long years working my tail off, first trying to raise cattle, then farming. What did I have to show for it? Nothing. I'd lost my place to the bank. In fact, I still owed Mr. Andrews, who owned the bank, three hundred dollars.

Since the sheriff's job wasn't too demanding, I'd been helping out down at Mr. Burdett's blacksmith shop a couple of afternoons a week. I hoped to earn enough extra money to pay Andrews the money owed.

My eyes threatening to close, I tipped my head

back, leaning my chair against the building. Just as I was about to sink into a good little nap, I heard the rumbling of a wagon coming down the street. I cocked open one eye, casting a lazy glance down the street. When I saw old man Wiesmulluer sittin' in the middle of that wagon, I durn near split my britches, I snapped up so fast.

Jerking my hat down, I slapped a dignified expression on my face, trying to look like I was a sentinel guarding the town from potential wrongdoers. I reacted that way partly because old man Wiesmulluer was such a grouchy ol' cuss who didn't hold with lazing about, and partly because of Betsy. I reckon Betsy Wiesmulluer was about the most beautiful creature I ever did see.

I waved at the whole bunch as they went by, but only Mrs. Wiesmulluer and Edwina waved back. The old man didn't even look over, and Betsy just gave me a cool, aloof glance.

My face burning hot, I watched as they pulled up in front of the store. My heart pounded in my chest as Betsy stepped gracefully down from the wagon. Where Betsy glided down, her sister Edwina simply jumped, landing lightly on her feet.

I tell you them two girls were about alike as daylight and dark. Where Betsy was tall and willowy, Edwina was shorter, with a bouncy, lively step. Instead of the long flowing blonde hair like Betsy's, Edwina's hair was black as midnight.

Making sure no dust had settled on my bright new badge, I hitched up my britches and rared my shoulders back. Walking slowly and with the dignity befitting a man of my position, I crossed the street.

"Did Burdett get my wheels finished?" Wiesmulluer asked, referring to some wagon wheels he left at the blacksmith shop to be repaired.

"Yes, sir, we finished them yesterday," I replied, looking past him to where Betsy stood leaning against the front wall of the store. "I could fetch them over here if you want."

Wiesmulluer had started inside, but now he turned back. "I'd be obliged," he said, but his tone said that I should have just done it without needing to ask.

I nodded, tipping my hat to the ladies, trying to work up the nerve to say something and failing miserably. Disgusted and sore at myself, I dogged up to the combination livery stable and blacksmith shop. I knew Edwina was following me, but I tried to ignore her.

"Are you going to the dance on Saturday?" Edwina asked.

"I reckon I have to, it's part of my job, Eddy," I said gruffly.

"You don't seem too excited about it," she observed.

"Not much goes on at them things but fighting and dancing," I said, leaving out the drinking— there was plenty of that too. "Nobody will dance with me, not after I stepped on Mrs. Claude's foot that time," I said, ducking my head, ashamed of the memory. "Mrs. Claude limped for a week after I mashed her foot."

"I'd dance with you, if you ask me," Edwina said, with a lot of spunk. "I'm real quick on my feet. I can dodge them big shoes of yours," she said, laughing at me.

I only grunted, sore at her for making fun of me. Burdett looked up from his forge as we approached. "Mr. Wiesmulluer wants his wheels," I explained, going to where we had them stacked.

"I figured he'd be in for them today," Burdett replied, tipping his hat to Eddy. "How are you today, Eddy?"

"I'm just fine, Mr. Burdett, how about yourself?" Eddy asked cheerfully, and I groaned, cutting my eyes toward the sky. Burdett was a good man, but he always had half a dozen things ailing him.

"Not so good, Eddy. I sure been feeling poorly." While Burdett listed all the things bothering him on this day, I drug out the wheels. Running my arms through the spokes, I picked up two with each hand.

"You need some help with those, Teddy?" Edwina asked, hurrying over, eager to lend a hand.

"No, I got them," I said, and I reckon I must have been a bit gruff, judging from the hurt look that came to her black eyes. Feeling ashamed, I ducked my head and took off, lugging them wheels up the street. I mean, I liked Eddy, but she sure could be a nuisance sometimes.

Eddy caught up to me, but she didn't speak as we returned to her father's wagon. As I piled them wheels in the wagon, my eyes strayed toward the store, trying to see inside. I longed for another glimpse of Betsy. Finally, I decided I best go inside and tell Wiesmulluer that I had his wheels loaded.

Jerking my gunbelt up, I walked inside, searching the store for Betsy. She and Mrs. Wiesmulluer stood in the back of the store, sorting through a pile of women's foofaraw.

"You get them wheels loaded?" Wiesmulluer barked, sounding sore. "Tell Burdett that I'll be needing them horseshoes in the next couple of days," he added, without giving me a chance to answer his first question.

"Yes sir," I answered, my eyes drifting to the back of the store. Sometimes, I wondered why Betsy couldn't be more like Eddy. I couldn't get Eddy to leave me alone, and I couldn't even get Betsy to give me a second glance.

"This ain't no way to run a business," Wiesmulluer grumbled, struggling to tally up his purchases. "I don't know why that fool Gid can't stay in here and run this place proper, instead of spending all his time in the saloon."

"Yes, sir," I said, not knowing what else to say.

"You still here? I thought I told you to go get Burdett busy on my horseshoes," Wiesmulluer barked.

"I'm on my way," I said, taking a last look at Betsy.

My thoughts on Betsy, I shuffled down to the livery.

"Mr. Wiesmulluer said you should get busy on his shoes," I told Burdett.

"What do you think I am working on now?" Burdett asked, sounding irritated. "You coming down to help me tomorrow?"

"Yeah, I suppose so."

"What are you so moon-eyed about? You been looking at that Betsy girl again?"

"Yeah," I answered, feeling myself grin stupidly.

Burdett swore and spat in the dust. "Old man Wiesmulluer catches you even looking at that girl and he'll barbecue your backside," Burdett warned, shaking his head. "That badge you're wearing won't make no never mind to him."

"But she sure is pretty," I said, with a sigh.

Burdett snorted. ''Purty ain't what's important,'' he said. ''Can she cook, clean, and take care of you? That's the important thing.''

''I suppose,'' I agreed, but I wasn't really listening.

As he talked, four men thundered up the street, choking us with their dust as they pounded past. One of the men was a big man, almost as big as me. One of them had long blonde hair, one was redheaded, and the other a skinny devil. All in all, they were a salty-looking bunch.

Scratching my chin, I watched as they dismounted in front of the saloon. Beating the dust from their clothes, they walked inside. Now, I'm the sheriff, and part of my job is to check out strangers, so I decided I'd best head up to the saloon and see what was going on.

''I've got to go,'' I said, cutting into Burdett's ramblings. ''I'll be by in the morning to give you a hand,'' I promised, hitching up my gunbelt. Rubbing my hands together, I walked up the street. The moment I stepped into the saloon, I sensed something wasn't right.

The smiling man sat at the poker table, his back against the wall. He was playing cards with Gid Stevens and Mr. Andrews. From the expression on his face, I figured the stranger was winning.

My eyes traveled from the card game to the men at the bar. The four strangers were the only ones at the bar. They stood quietly drinking their beers, looking into the back bar mirror. Nothing wrong with that, but I still felt that something was out of place.

Maybe it was the fact that so many strangers were in town. After all, it wasn't often that strangers came to Whiskey City. I figured it my duty to keep an eye on things, so I shouldered past the four strangers, making my way down to the far end of the bar.

Knowing what I'd be wanting, the bartender carried a beer down to me. "Thanks, Joe," I said, tossing him a coin. Sipping my beer, I divided my attention between the smiling stranger at the card table and the four gents at the bar.

I noticed the four men at the bar whispering among themselves. Every once in a while, one of them would raise his head up and glare in my direction, then duck and go to whispering again. All of a sudden, the big man silenced the whispering with a swipe of his meaty hand. Pushing away from the others, he stalked over to the card table. He stood there, drinking his beer and watching the play.

"What are you doing here, Stamper?" he asked suddenly.

The stranger looked up from his cards, appraising the big man. The flashing smile still rode on Stamper's face, but I noticed his eyes looked like a blizzard blowing in from the north. "If it's any of your business, Butch, I'm taking a lesson in the fine art of poker from these fine gentlemen."

Big ol' Butch rocked on his heels, sipping his beer and studying the man he called Stamper. Dark color shot up Butch's neck and face. He bowed his shoulders and hunched over, reminding me of a bull about to charge.

The men who rode into town with Butch eased away from the bar, forming a half circle in front of the poker table. If the stranger noticed the maneuver or was worried about it, he hid it well. His hands were steady as he carelessly flipped a chip into the pot.

Butch stabbed at Stamper with a tree trunk finger. "I don't like you being here," Butch challenged.

Stamper acted like he never even heard as he calmly tossed down the winning hand, three tens. Without bothering to look at Butch, Stamper raked in his winnings.

Right 'bout then, I didn't know what to do. If Butch and Stamper had a quarrel to settle, I didn't reckon it was my place to step in, not as long as it was a fair fight. The trouble was, I felt certain that if Butch started anything, them three goons were going to jump right in the middle of it.

'Course, after taking a second look at Stamper, I wondered if them three buying in might just about even up the odds. Stamper looked like a mighty cool character. I'd bet he could handle himself.

Then I saw something that brought my blood to a boil. That scrawny fella was sneaking for a hideout gun he had stashed behind his back. I shot a glance at Stamper, but he was looking at the blond-haired feller and Butch. Stamper didn't see the scrawny one going for the hideout gun.

As his greasy fingers tickled the butt of that pistol, my own hand dove for my pistol. As my hand closed around the butt of my pistol, that skinny feller begin drawing his gun.

I jerked on my pistol, but nothing happened. I'd plumb forgot to loosen the thong that held the gun in the holster.

My mouth hanging open, I watched as ol' Skinny pulled his gun.

Chapter Two

That scrawny feller had his gun out, already swinging it into firing position before I reacted. Without thinking, I snatched him by the neck. My big hand almost completely circling his throat, I jerked him clean off the floor. With my free hand, I clubbed his wrist, knocking the gun from his fist. Just for good measure, I batted him in the whiskers a couple of times.

By that time, Stamper had things well in hand. When I grabbed that skinny fella, Stamper had been sitting there, smiling at them, but now his smiling face looked over the barrel of a pistol.

Butch and the rest of his men stood flat-footed, their hands halfway to their guns. "Go ahead, try it," Stamper sneered as he rose slowly to his feet. "You know, Butch, I never did like you. I always figured you were a yellow dog," Stamper taunted.

Now, if I thought Butch looked like a bull before, he really did now. He pawed the floor, his big chest heaving and his nostrils flaring.

Stamper grinned tauntingly, daring Butch to try something. "If you don't like me being here, that's tough. I plan on staying a couple of days," Stamper allowed, his teeth flashing white against his skin. He cocked his head, looking at the ceiling. "Yeah, a couple of days ought to be plenty of time for me to do what I came here for."

"You stay here, and they will bury you here!" Butch threatened, his voice coming out in a choking rasp.

Butch's threat didn't faze Stamper, not in the least. He calmly reached down with his left hand and took up his drink. His eyes mocking, Stamper raised his glass and took a drink. For a second, I thought Butch was going to explode. His already red face turned almost black, and a choking sound rumbled from his throat.

I sucked in a deep breath, wondering how I could stop this. I thought about clobbering Butch once, just to slow him down, but then he let out a big sigh and his shoulders sagged.

Thinking the trouble was over, I'd just started to relax when the redhaired feller grabbed my arm. "Sheriff, for God's sake, you're going to choke him to death!"

A bit peeved at Red for butting in, I scowled at him, then glanced at Skinny. Sure enough, his face was beginning to turn a mite purple. His tongue lagged out of the side of his mouth, and his eyes bugled out of their sockets a good two inches.

Now maybe Red was right, but I figured this was law business and didn't take it kindly that he should butt in. Just to learn him a lesson, I swatted him alongside the head. I just gave him a little tap, but from the way he sailed back across that barroom, you'd thought he had a kite in the seat of his britches.

I sat Skinny down on the floor, giving him a shove in the direction of the door. Skinny wobbled a few steps, then fell in a pile beside his partner, Red.

Done with them two, I turned my attention to Butch and that blonde-haired fellow. Butch was pawing the floor and frothing at the mouth, but that blond fellow looked plumb calm. "I don't know you gents, but I don't take to the way you do business. Maybe after a long, hot ride, you'll realize the error in your ways," I said, doing my best to look like I meant business.

Butch, he muscled up like he was going to take on the whole saloon, but blondy grabbed him by the arm. "Forget it, Butch, there will be another time," he said, leading the big man to the door.

Butch frothed at the mouth and did some cussing, but he let that blonde man drag him out the door. Doing some grumbling themselves, Red and Skinny climbed to their feet and followed. Skinny was still huffing and puffing, and I noticed a big bruise already coming on his neck—not that I felt sorry for them; they came in looking for trouble and they sure enough found it.

Stamper waited until they were out the door, then flipped his pistol back in the holster. "Thanks for pitching in," he said, holding out his hand as he circled around the card table. "What's your name, Sheriff? I'd like to buy you a beer."

"Ted Cooper," I replied, taking his hand. "Who were those guys and why did they want to kill you?" I asked, trying to keep my thoughts on business and not free beer.

"The big man is Butch Adkins. The blonde man

is Dave Hetfield. The skinny one is Dean Charlton, and Red's name is Jake Baldwin,'' Stamper answered, paying for our beers.

"And what would your name be?" I pressed, taking the beer he offered.

He had his glass to his lips, and he looked over the top of it, hesitating a full second. "Stamper. Bobby Stamper," he said, then tipped his glass, taking a long drink.

Bobby Stamper! Yeah, I'd heard of him. Way I heard it, Bobby Stamper stole more money than a thousand crooked bankers put together. I'd also heard that he could open any lock ever made, and do it in the dark, with one hand behind his back.

The banker, Mr. Andrews, shot to his feet, looking like a lamb caught in a wolf's den.

"What brings you to Whiskey City?" I asked, watching the beer foam as I swirled it in my mug.

Stamper grinned, shrugging his shoulders. "Just passing through, looking for a nice quiet place to rest up for a spell," he announced cheerfully.

His face sagging with relief, Andrews slumped back into his chair, still chalk white from the scare. Well, maybe Andrews was satisfied with Stamper's answer, but I was not.

"You told Butch you had business in town. Business that would take a couple of days," I reminded him.

If I expected Stamper to look ashamed that he had been caught in a lie, I was in for a big disappointment. His face exploded in a big grin as he slapped me across the back. "You're right, that's sure enough what I told them." He looked Andrews straight in the eye. "Who knows, maybe I came here to rob your bank."

I shot a glance at Andrews, who didn't look so

relaxed now. Fact is, he looked like he was about to have an apoplexy. I wanted to chuckle; I never did care for the old skinflint, and since he was the one who closed out my farm, I had a hard time getting worked up over his troubles. Anyway, Andrews was always bragging on this fancy safe he had. ''No one in the world can open that safe without the combination, and I'm the only one with the combination. That money couldn't be safer if it was on the moon,'' Andrews was always saying.

Judging from the way his Adam's apple was bouncing up and down, the banker didn't look that sure about his lockbox now. I'd bet he would sleep in the bank till Stamper left town.

''Don't fret, I never came here to rob your bank,'' Stamper promised solemnly. Now his face and tone may have been solemn, but a daring deviltry danced in his eyes. Cocking his head off to one side, he scratched his chin. ''I heard you got one of them Harper-Evans boxes.''

Looking just about as comfortable as a man sittin' barebottomed on an anthill, Andrews swallowed a couple of times, then finally nodded.

''That wouldn't be the sixty-eight model? The six-footer with the double locks?''

Hanging on to the edge of the table for support, Andrews managed another weak nod. That mocking light still sparkling in his eyes, Stamper looked at the ceiling and rubbed the side of his neck. ''I don't know,'' he said, shaking his head slowly. ''I heard them sixty-eights are mighty near impossible to crack.'' All pretense of seriousness dropped from Stamper's face as he looked Andrews square in the eye. ''I might have to pry open that safe of yours, just to show that it can be done!''

Andrews shot to his feet, his whole face quivering with rage. ''Sheriff, arrest this man!''

''What for?'' Stamper asked, spreading his hands in front of him and looking innocent as a newborn colt.

''We've all heard you rob banks for a living,'' I said, drawing myself up to my full height. Now maybe I didn't care for Andrews, but I was the sheriff of Whiskey City, a job I took real serious. If Stamper meant to rob the bank, then I'd put a stop to it.

''You heard I was a bank robber? Well, I've heard tell of a fat gent that lives at the North Pole and goes by the name of Santy Claus, but that don't make him real,'' Stamper said, a slight jeering note in his voice.

''You're right about that,'' I admitted. ''Maybe I don't have no call to arrest you, but I can sure keep an eye on you.''

Stamper laughed, finishing his beer. ''You do that, Sheriff. As a matter of fact, you can watch me have another beer.'' Stamper hesitated, looking at me out of the corner of his eye. ''You want one?''

I surely did. I mean, all this law business tended to give me a parched throat, but I figured if I was going to match wits with a smooth character like Stamper, I'd best have a clear head. ''No thanks,'' I told him.

''Suit yourself,'' Stamper replied, shrugging his shoulders. He turned to the bar, shouting at Joe to bring him another beer. ''What's that all about?'' he asked, gesturing to the jar of money and the wooden scoreboard.

''A couple of fellers get into a scrap every so often. The board's there to keep track of who won the most fights. The money in the jar is what's already been bet on the next fight. Every time Wiesmulluer and Claude get together, they go to scrapping. Most times, things go to popping before anyone can get ready, so folks took to preparing before hand,'' I told him.

''Now, that's downright inconsiderate of them if you ask me,'' Stamper commented. ''You'd think that the least they could do is give a man time to place a friendly wager or two.''

I shrugged. Betting wasn't exactly in my line. I had to scrap and claw to get ahold of a dollar, and I wasn't about to take a chance on losing it.

''Folks say this town came to be when them two got into their first fight. They went to battling, and folks naturally gathered around to watch, and when the dust settled, there was a town. An old trapper named Turley Simmons came riding up, and seeing all the folks, he thought this was some kind of great city. He asked if there was any whiskey in this city, and the town had a name.''

For a minute while I rambled on, the smile left Stamper's face. ''You know Turley Simmons?'' he asked, sounding mighty casual.

''Sure, I know him,'' I replied, wondering what Turley meant to Stamper. Stamper seemed to be just making conversation, but I done enough fishing to know when something was nibbling on my hook.

I shrugged, taking the last sip of my beer. ''I reckon everybody in town knows Turley. He comes to town once or twice a year, spends a month or so just lazing around and swapping stories,'' I said, watching Stamper's face.

His smile was back. ''I was just wondering. Turley is some distant kin of mine,'' he said easily.

I wasn't sure I bought all of that, but I let it drop. I sure didn't believe all that about being in town just to rest up. Stamper didn't strike me as the sitting-around type. He had something in mind, I'd bet on that.

I wasn't forgetting about Butch Adkins and his bunch either. They looked rough as porcupine fur to me. I just knew they were up to no good. I had a feeling that trouble was brewing just around the bend.

That Stamper was becoming more confusing by the minute. Three days had passed, and I was beginning to change my mind about Bobby Stamper. Maybe he was the sitting-around type after all, 'cause all he did was sit in the saloon, playing cards and telling some of the biggest whoppers I ever did hear—that and purely torment Mr. Andrews.

Stamper seemed to take real joy in making life miserable for the banker. Myself, I enjoyed watching it, but a couple of times, I had to remind myself that Stamper was an outlaw and needed watching.

The first day, Stamper went down to the bank, asking Andrews to bust up a twenty-dollar gold piece. Sweat poured off the banker while he made the change, and from where I stood, I could see the quiver in his hands.

Acting all unconcerned, Stamper raised up on his toes, looking over Andrew's shoulder to where the big safe stood in the corner behind the counter. "Is that the Harper-Evans?" Stamper asked innocently.

"Yes," Andrews replied, sounding nervous as he bobbed around, trying to block Stamper's view of the safe.

"It sure is a beauty," Stamper said, whistling softly. "Do you mind if I take a look at it?"

"Yes, I do mind!" Andrews snapped, shoving Stamper's change at him. "Here's your money. Take it and go; I'm a very busy man."

"I can see that," Stamper replied dryly as he glanced about the empty bank. "You should learn to be more polite to potential customers. I was thinking I might do some business at this bank," Stamper said, then grinned wickedly. "I had in mind to make a withdrawal."

Red flamed to Andrews' face and he gripped the counter so hard I though he might snap a chunk of it off. I chuckled to myself as Stamper gave Andrews a small salute, then walked out of the bank.

Stamper stood just outside the bank, lighting a cigar as I came out. "That banker sure is a nervous-acting cuss," Stamper commented, waving the match out. "Why, you'd think he never seen a real live bank robber before."

The next day Stamper strolled into the bank and shoved a wad of his poker winnings at Andrews. "Mr. Andrews, I've decided to open an account in your fine establishment," Stamper announced, slapping his hand on the counter.

Andrews looked from the pile of money to Stamper's face, then back to the money. With a greedy smile flickering across his face, Andrews licked his lips and pulled the money to him. He counted the money, whipping through the stack faster than I could believe.

"I came up with seventy-two dollars and thirty-six cents," Andrews said, looking up with a question in his eyes, smiling as Stamper nodded in agreement. "Would you like a receipt, Mr. Stamper?"

Stamper allowed that he would, leaning against the counter while Andrews scrawled a receipt on a piece of paper. ''You know, Mr. Andrews, it appears to me that this bank ain't safe.''

Andrews's head snapped up so fast that he jerked the pen across the receipt, making a big mark across it. Swearing viciously, Andrews crumpled up the receipt and threw it across the room. ''What do you mean?'' he asked, his voice a mite strained.

''That window there,'' Stamper replied, waving a careless hand at the window over Mr. Andrews's desk.

''What about it?'' Andrews growled, starting on a new receipt.

''Well, it occurs to me that an enterprising young man might sneak down the alley some night, force open the window, and rob this establishment.''

I saw the faint sheen of sweat on Andrews' face as he looked back at the window. ''That's what we hired him for,'' Andrews muttered, pointing to where I stood, leaning against the front wall of the bank.

''And a fine choice you made,'' Stamper agreed, craning his neck to watch as Andrews worked on the new receipt. ''But the good sheriff can't be everywhere at once. I'm sure there are times when he has to be out of town. Say, if someone lost some cows, the sheriff would have to go check it out and track down the rustlers.''

''I have the best safe ever made,'' Andrews said, handing the receipt to Stamper, who wadded it into a ball, carelessly cramming the paper into his pocket.

''That you do,'' Stamper agreed heartily. ''And if you don't mind, I'll wait until you put my money in the safe. These days a body can't be too careful. I wouldn't want to take a chance on losing it.''

I swear Andrews actually groaned, but he never

argued with Stamper. Scooping up the pile of money, the banker carried it back to the safe. He sure looked funny as he humped over in front of the locks, trying to make sure Stamper couldn't see what numbers he turned. It took him a long time to open the box, since he kept looking back over his shoulder, making certain that Stamper wasn't peeking.

Stamper for his part seemed awful unconcerned with the whole procedure. He idly watched out the window, every once in a while grinning back at me. "Are you having trouble with the safe, Mr. Andrews?" Stamper asked, his voice ringing with orneriness. "I could give you a hand if you like."

"I'll manage," Andrews growled, and I bet he was thinking the same thing I was—that Stamper could probably open that box a lot faster.

Finally, Andrews pried the door open and shoved Stamper's wad inside. "There you go, Mr. Stamper, all safe and sound. Now, is there anything else I can do for you?"

"No, that's fine. When I need the money, I'll be back to get it."

I followed Stamper from the bank, having truly enjoyed watching Andrews squirm. One thing you had to say about Bobby Stamper, he sure knew how to liven things up.

"I sure would like to see my uncle, Turley Simmons," Stamper said out of the blue. "How often does he come to town?"

"Not often," I replied with a shrug. "You never can tell when he's going to show up."

"Does he have a place around here, or does he usually stay in the hotel?"

"You know, I don't rightly know," I said, taking my hat off and scratching my head. "I just took the job as sheriff. Before that, I was a farmer and didn't spend too much time in town. 'Bout the only place I ever saw Turley was the saloon. I kinda got the feeling he stayed there most of the time.''

"Is that so?'' Stamper said, more to himself than me. Rubbing his chin, he walked into the hotel.

The next morning was Saturday, and I stood out in front of the jail watching Andrews cart a raft of boards up to the bank. The banker was nailing them over the window when Stamper came out of the hotel. He walked boldly to where I stood outside the jail. "I'm going for a little ride and since you're going to trail me, why don't you ride along and keep me company?'' he invited, sporting a daring grin.

I started to decline, my hackles rising at his attitude, but then I shrugged. Riding with him sure would beat slinking along behind in the bushes. "Let me fetch my horse,'' I told him.

A few minutes later, we rode side by side out of town. Leaning back in the saddle, Stamper pushed back his hat and begin building a smoke. "You know, I don't think that I thanked you right and proper for stepping in and lending me a hand the other day,'' he said.

"You bought me a beer. That's about the best way to say thanks that I know of.''

Stamper chuckled, poking the smoke into his mouth. "Still, I am obliged. You surely did save me a pile of grief,'' he said, holding a match to his cigarette. "You move pretty fast for such a big man, but next time, I suggest that you slip the thong off that pistol.''

I felt my face coloring at the memory. "I seen the trouble coming, but I forgot,'' I admitted.

"Well, I must say, you did pretty good with just

your bare hands," he observed dryly. "You ever have to use that pistol much?" he asked, pulling his horse to a stop.

"No. Except for a little hunting and practicing, that would have been the first time."

Stamper nodded, kicking his leg over the saddlehorn and sliding off his horse. He tied the animal, draping his saddlebags over his shoulder, then walked over to the creek. He slid down to the bottom of the dry stream. Wondering what he was up to now, I kicked loose from my saddle and followed. Just up the creek a piece, I could see the pond locally know as Miller's Hole.

From the saddlebags, Stamper took a bunch of bottles. Whistling softly, he lined the bottles up against the creek bank. "Let's see you shoot," he suggested.

I followed him across the creek, eyeing them bottles with the utmost concentration. I had a sneaky feeling that Bobby Stamper could put a bullet through the eye of a needle, and I didn't want to embarrass myself.

Backing off about twenty paces, I drug out my pistol and banged off a shot. To my relief, one of the bottles exploded, and danged if it wasn't the one I aimed at.

My chest puffing out, I rammed my pistol down in the holster and glanced over at Stamper. "That was pretty good," he admitted. "Can you do it fast? Like this?"

In the blink of an eye, he drew and fired. The bullet sawed the neck right off one bottle. Grinning broadly, Stamper dropped his gun in the holster, then jerked it back out, firing and smashing the bottle dead center.

"Saves bottles that way," he explained. Not that

I was sure I believed him, I figure he missed his first shot slightly. "You try one fast," he suggested.

Jerking my hat down, I stared at the row of bottles, rubbing my hands together. Suddenly, I made a swipe at my pistol. I was jerking it out of the holster, when the dang thing went off! I swear, it nearly blowed my whole foot off, the bullet striking the ground inches in front of my toes. Yelping, I jumped backward, tangling my spurs.

I ended up flat on my back with Stamper standing over me. "I reckon that shot was a mite low," he said, serious like.

Growling, I batted away the hand he extended down to me. Determined, I shoved myself to my feet, checking to make sure all my parts were still together.

"You need a little more practice, that's all," Stamper said. "Here, watch me again." Once more, he whipped up his pistol and broke the neck off a bottle.

"How in the blazes am I supposed to watch and see how you do it? Everything is just a blur," I grumbled.

"Don't worry, you'll get the hang of it," Stamper said, chuckling.

Using the sleeve of my shirt, I wiped the sweat from my face and set my feet firmly in the sand. Sticking my tongue out, I eyed them bottles. I dove for my pistol, pulling her cleanly from the holster this time. I leveled the gun and squeezed the trigger. The bullet missed the bottles, smacking into a flat rock behind them, ricocheting wildly. I flinched as the bullet screamed back past us, sounding like a cat with a mashed tail.

"That's better, but you're turning your body as

you draw. That's throwing your aim off,'' Stamper told me.

We worked at it a long time, and by the time we quit, I could snatch my pistol and fire, hitting one of the bottles every now and again.

Reloading my gun, I followed Stamper back to where we left the horses. ''If you are planning to rob our bank, why are you taking the trouble to help me shoot better?'' I asked.

''Who said I was planning to rob your bank?''

''You did,'' I answered. ''You said you were hankering to take a crack at that fancy safe of Andrews.''

''Oh yeah, I did say that,'' Stamper agreed, sporting a daring grin. ''Maybe I just don't want to kill a greenhorn like you.''

I didn't say anything, and for once, Stamper turned serious. ''No, I reckon the reason is that you saved my bacon in the saloon the other day.''

Stamper swung up on his horse, rubbing his chin as he watched me jerk my cinch tight. ''One at a time, I could have handled them boys, although Hetfield is very good. All together, they would have salted me away.''

''As long as you're being truthful, why don't you tell me about the bank? Are you going to rob it?''

Stamper's grin was both wide and immediate. ''I ain't rightly decided. I always did want to take a crack at one of those sixty-eights, though.''

We rode to town, neither of us saying much. ''I hear they are having some kind of dance tonight,'' Stamper commented, watching as some of the folks set up benches behind the church.

''That's right,'' I said, tight-lipped. For some reason, I didn't want him to go to the dance.

"Well, if I'm going to this party, I better have a nap this afternoon," Stamper decided.

I didn't bother answering. I promised Mr. Burdett that I would help him with the shoes for Wiesmulluer's horses, and it was high time I got after it.

"Good morning, Mr. Burdett," I said, tying my horse in front of the barn.

"I don't know what's so good about it," Burdett complained sourly. "My gout's been acting up, and I'm a week behind. You was supposed to help me with Wiesmulluer's shoes. If we don't get them done today, he'll throw a fit."

"I meant to get down here sooner, but I've been busy with law business."

"Law business," Burdett snorted. "You call what you've been doing law business? All you've done is follow that Stamper character around."

"Stamper is a known man, and he practically said he was going to rob the bank," I said defensively.

Burdett shook his head, dunking a finished shoe in the water barrel. "Aw, Bobby ain't gonna rob us. He seems like a right nice young man to me. I 'spect that all them stories about him are just tall tales. Anyway, everybody knows that nobody can open that safe of Andrews's."

I didn't want to argue, so I kept my mouth shut and went to work. We worked all afternoon, hammering them shoes into shape. We were working on the last set when Wiesmulluer's wagon rumbled into town.

Shielding my eyes from the sun, I watched as the wagon rolled by. "Quit your gawking at that yeller-haired gal and get back to work," Burdett instructed.

I did as Burdett wished, but I couldn't keep my mind off her. I messed up one shoe because I was daydreaming about her. Burdett howled like a coon tracking a scent when he saw the ruined shoe.

I imagine he would have given me quite the rawhiding, but lo and behold if Betsy herself didn't walk up to the shop. "Father asked me to check and see if you had his shoes ready," she said.

"Just finishing up now," Burdett assured.

"Good. We're staying in town tonight, but Father will want to pick them up tomorrow."

"That'd be just fine," Burdett said, but I doubt if he was happy about having to come down and load the shoes on Sunday.

Betsy turned toward me, holding her hands behind her back and looking up at me. "Are you going to the dance tonight, Teddy?" she asked, dancing lightly from one foot to the other.

"I have to be there just to make sure no one starts any trouble," I said, squaring my shoulders back.

"Well, be sure to save me a dance," Betsy said, giving me a smile as bright and pretty as a sunny day.

Unable to speak, I nodded my head, watching her as she turned and walked up the street. I watched her until she disappeared into the store. Surprisingly, she turned and gave me a small wave before going inside.

Burdett straightened up, rubbing the small of his back. "I can see I won't get any work out of you now. You might as well run along," Burdett said, groaning. "It's no wonder my back bothers me, I can't keep good help. I swear, young folks these days, they don't know the meaning of work. . . . "

I suppose Burdett said some more. When he gets

off on one of his kicks, he usually rambles on and on. Course, this time if he had some more to say, he was talking to himself.

I hustled up the street, heading for the hotel. I fixed me a bath, scrubbing my hide till it was red and half raw. Deciding I was clean enough, I dressed, putting on clean clothes. My throat dry and my palms sweating, I lumbered down to the church, feeling as out of place as a muddy hog in a fancy parlor.

I stopped in front of the church, taking a minute to slick back my hair before I went around back to where they were having the dance. The fiddlers were playing, but most folks were sitting on benches, eating from baskets and just visiting. Feeling like a complete fool, I was ready to bolt and run when Eddy Wiesmulluer bounced over to me. The smile she gave made me feel jumpy inside and set my feet to shuffling.

"Teddy, do you want something to eat? We have plenty," Eddy offered.

"No, I'm not hungry," I said, then regretted it. I was a mite on the hungry side. "Lots of folks here," I said, jamming my hands down in my pockets.

"They came from everywhere I guess," Eddy replied. "We saw horses and buggies going by the house all day."

"Parties are rare. I don't reckon anyone wanted to miss this one."

My eyes had been roaming the crowd, hoping for a glimpse of Betsy, and when I saw her, she was gliding toward me. "Hi, Teddy," Betsy said, exchanging a cool look with Eddy. Although they were sisters, they never seemed to get along.

"You promised to dance with me," Betsy said, holding her hand out to me.

This was the moment I'd been dreaming of, I'd prayed for. My heart was thumping so hard, I was afraid it would jump right out of my chest.

Betsy held my hand, leading me out in the clearing. Already, a few couples were out there whooping it up. Betsy looked back at me, giving me a smile that almost melted my heart.

I slipped my arm around her waist and she stepped up close. "Do you know that new guy in town, Bobby Stamper?" Betsy asked.

"Yeah, I met him," I said, not wanting to talk about him.

"I heard he's a bank robber. That sounds so exciting," Betsy said, her voice sounding dreamy.

We didn't get to finish our dance, as a loud crash sounded, followed by a stream of high-pitched French cuss words. Right in the middle of the song, the fiddlers dropped their instruments, rushing over to see the fight.

Wiesmulluer and Claude were squared off, ready to get after it, when Mrs. Wiesmulluer stepped between them. Her dark eyes flashing pure fire, Marie Wiesmulluer pushed her husband back. "Karl Wiesmulluer! If you think I'm going to stand here and watch you ruin another pleasant evening with your temper, you've got another think coming."

Mrs. Wiesmulluer crossed her arms, staring defiantly at her husband. "You apologize to Mr. Claude and give him your hand."

Wiesmulluer backed up, his square jaw setting firm. "Apologize to Claude? Never! Now, get out of my way while I teach this French whelp a lesson!"

Mrs. Wiesmulluer stood her ground, not at all

intimidated by all of Wiesmulluer's blustering. She just glared at him until his eyes fell and his head bowed. I think the old man was ready to back down, when Claude let out a snicker.

Claude started to say something, but his wife cuffed him across the back of the head. "Louie, shut up and shake Mr. Wiesmulluer's hand."

They never shook hands, but they backed away snapping and growling like a couple of stray dogs. I swear, you could feel the disappointment of the crowd.

Slowly folks went about their business, griping about not getting to see the long-awaited fight. While the fiddlers started back up, I cast about, looking for Betsy. Now, where had that girl gone to?

"Teddy, are you ready to dance?" Eddy asked. "You promised."

I guess I did promise, so I followed Eddy, but my eyes kept scanning for Betsy. Eddy chatted the whole time we danced, only stopping when I accidently stepped on her foot. We'd got to going faster than I was used to, and she shoulda had the sense to keep her feet back. As we was walking back to the benches, I saw Betsy. She was walking, her arm around Bobby Stamper!

For a second, my whole body went stiff and cold. Then a red-hot anger flashed through me. "I've got to go, Eddy," I said, and bolted after Betsy.

I ran around the church, skidding to a halt in the middle of the street. I glanced up and down the street, but it looked to be deserted. Like an angry bull, I paced back and forth, snorting and pawing the ground. Then I saw a one-horse buggy pull out of the alley and head slowly from town.

Running hard, I sprinted down to the barn, catching up my horse and slapping the saddle on his back. By the time I rode out of the barn, the buggy had disappeared.

Slapping the spurs to my horse, I galloped down the road after it. We rode hard for a couple of miles before I caught sight of the buggy. It was parked on the edge of the road, by Miller's Hole. Sliding my horse to a stop, I dropped the reins and jumped to the ground.

I could see two people inside the buggy, sitting very close. As I watched, I saw them lean close, their lips coming together. A fearful rage welled up inside me and, letting loose a mighty roar, I charged the buggy!

Chapter Three

I charged down that slope, roaring like a lion with a toothache. I hit that buggy broadside with a full head of steam behind me. When I slammed into that light buggy, it flipped over like a poker chip. My mouth gaping open in amazement, I watched as it tumbled over the edge of the bank, dragging horse and all into the pond.

That buggy hit the water, sending a splash high into the air. I stood back, unable to suppress a feeling of satisfaction. I mean, I didn't like it that I went and got so mad, but I couldn't deny that I enjoyed tossing that buggy into the water.

My rosy feeling faded as a squawky female voice cut loose with a string of cussing like I never heard before. Now, I couldn't place the voice, but I knew one thing—it wasn't the sweet tone of Betsy Wiesmulluer.

The horse drawing the buggy scrambled up the bank and took out for town like a house on fire, jerking the light buggy behind. I had to jump out of the road as the horse thundered by, and by the time I climbed back to my feet, I could see a pair of folks struggling in the water. Judging by the amount of cussin' coming from the pond, they weren't happy either.

Even in the gloom, I could see a woman standing in the waist-deep water, splashing water twenty feet into the air as she struggled to make it across the pond. A man scurried along behind her, doing his best to help her, but every time he touched her, she slapped his hand away. Just for good measure, she clouted him upside the head with a little clutch purse she had looped around her wrist with a drawstring.

Howling, the man waved his hands in the air, fighting for balance. All of a sudden, his feet shot out from underneath him, and he flipped over backward. He came up spitting, sputtering, and splashing water in every direction.

As she struggled out of the water, I recognized the woman, Iris Winkler! A bedraggled and funny-looking Mrs. Winkler, but that's sure enough who it was.

I was so stunned to see her out here, especially with a man, that I just stood there gaping at her with my mouth drooping wide open. Knowing that I'd went and stepped in it this time, I started to slink away 'fore they saw me.

"Theodore!"

I hunched my shoulders as Iris bawled out my name. Dang, I'd waited too long.

"Are you just going to stand there gawking like a dang dong fool, or are you going to help me out of the water?" Mrs. Winkler said, practically howling.

Let me tell you, she sure put me in motion.

Leaning out, I reached a hand down to her. She latched on to my hand, and I hauled her out of the water, her feet making sucking sounds as I jerked her clean out of the water and plopped her down on the bank.

"Let go of me, you big oaf!" she yelled, boxing my ears with that purse. She whacked me once more, adding a few choice words that liked to have shocked the life out of me. Why, I never heard such words . . . well, not since the day Mr. Burdett sat on his red-hot forge.

"Gid, I lost one of my shoes. Don't you come out of the water till you find it," Mrs. Winkler said, bawling out the order. Ol' Gid, he never argued, he just dove under the surface, and you can bet he never came up till he had that shoe.

Holding that shoe between his teeth, Gid half swum and half crawled over to the edge. Snaring him by the back of the collar, I hauled him up out of the water. Swinging him around, I plopped the old duffer down on the bank.

By the time me and Gid hustled up on the road, Iris was already there. She stood in the middle of the road, looking like a hornet's nest that's been kicked over. She had her hands on her hips, and I could just see mad poking out from every side of her.

If it hadn't been for the fact that she was so mad, I reckon I would have laughed, 'cause she sure was a funny-looking sight. Her good Sunday bonnet sat crooked on her head, a piece of moss hanging from it. Her stringy, iron gray hair stuck to her face.

Mrs. Winkler started to talk, her mouth working a couple of times before any words came out, but when they came, they roared out of her mouth with considerable wind power behind them.

"Theodore Cooper, what in the world has gotten into that thick skull of yours?" She stopped long enough to suck in a fresh charge of wind and push a mess of that hair outta her face. Then she grabbed me by the ear. She shook my head so hard, I thought it would come loose from my neck. "Have you lost what little mind you had?" she demanded, poking her face up to mine.

"I thought you was somebody else," I stammered, stumbling back a step or so.

"Who in creation did you think it might be?" she asked, then cut in before I had a chance to answer. "Not that it matters. Tell me, young man, do you always go around pushing unsuspecting people into the river? I swear, I don't know what gets into you young people these days."

"I'm real sorry about this, ma'am," I said, hanging my head. "My horse is right over yonder. Let me fetch him, and you and Mr. Stevens can ride him to town."

"Don't bother, we can manage very well on our own," she replied testily. From the way Gid's head snapped up, I reckon he would have liked the ride. It was a good couple of miles into town, and I doubt if Gid ever walked that far in his whole life.

"Let's go, Gid," Mrs. Winkler said, grabbing Gid by the arm and propelling him down the road with a healthy shove. I watched them walk away, feeling downright ashamed of myself. I didn't know quite what to do; I hated to mount up and ride past them.

Once, I saw Gid try to put his arm around her, and Iris gave him a sharp elbow in the short ribs. Even from where I stood, I could see Gid's shoulders hunch and hear him suck in a rasping breath.

My head sagging plumb down to my chest, I

shuffled over to where I left my horse. Leaning against the saddle, I patted his neck, feeling plumb sorry for myself. Here I'd went and made a complete fool out of myself over a woman that would barely speak to me.

'Course, if it hadn't been for that dang Bobby Stamper . . . Just when Betsy was starting to like me, he had to poke his nose into things. An anger began to build in me, and I had cursed his sorry hide. I made myself a promise that I would watch the ornery cuss's every move, and when he stepped out of line, which I knew he would, I'd slap his behind in jail so fast he'd have to wait a day for the rest of him to catch up.

Gritting my teeth in determination, I slapped the seat of my saddle. Dang right! That's exactly what I'd do. Gathering the reins, I vaulted into the saddle. Jerking my horse around, I spurred him for town.

It didn't take long to catch up with ol' widow Winkler and Gid. Old widow Winkler was really giving poor Gid the business for bringing her out here. She was giving me almost as much credit for their trouble, and believe me, I wouldn't want what she said repeated. Why, if she had been a man, I coulda shot her for saying such things. She even went so far as to compare my brain power to that of a Missouri mule.

My ears burning, I swung wide, circling around the pair, slinking into town like an alley cat.

The first person I saw as I rode into Whiskey City was Eddy Wiesmulluer. She stood outside the church, looking up to the sky with a wistful half-smile on her face. I pulled my horse up in the shadows of a couple of huge cottonwoods. As I watched her, it occurred to me that young Miss Edwina

Wiesmulluer was growing up to be a right hand-some young lady.

Although I don't know if lady was a word that rightly fit Eddy. She had way too much spunk and spirit to be a real lady. It came to me that if I hadn't let Eddy wrangle me into dancing with her, Stamper wouldn't have had the chance to slip off with Betsy.

Dang her, I thought, feeling a resentment toward her. My anger at Eddy was unreasoning, deep down, I knew that. The trouble was, I wanted to be mad at someone, and Eddy seemed like a likely choice.

"Are you going to sit out there all night scowling at me, or ride up and be sociable?" Eddy asked, nearly startling me out of my socks. Dang woman must have eyes like a bat. I never dreamed she could see me, pulled back in the shadows like I was.

Muttering to my horse, I touched a spur to his side. "You look like you been sucking on sour apples," Eddy commented, sounding mighty danged chipper about it. "It wouldn't kill you to smile."

Well, maybe not, but I didn't feel like smiling just then, especially not at her. "Where's Betsy?" I asked, my tone rough as tree bark.

For a second, Eddy looked like I pinched her in the side, then she smiled tiredly. "Off somewhere sparking with that outlaw fella, Bobby Stamper."

I grunted. Just like I figured. Well, one thing was dead dog certain, one of these days, I was going to fix Stamper's wagon, but good.

"Is that what's got your tail so twisted out of whack? Eddy asked. "I swear, I don't know why you chase after her so. Betsy's not the kind of woman you need."

"Yeah? What do you know about it?" I asked gruffly.

"A lot more than you think, Teddy Cooper!" she said, jabbing me in the gizzard with her finger. "And if you would stop walking around, acting as surly as a bear with a sore paw, you might see it."

"Aw, I'm sorry, Eddy," I said, realizing I'd went and made her angry, and feeling pretty low about it. "Don't mind me, it's just that I up and done something tonight that I'm awful ashamed of."

Eddy crossed her arms, giving me a right severe look. "Theodore Cooper, what fool thing have you done this time?"

I clamped my jaws shut, hanging my head. I meant to keep mum about giving widow Winkler and Gid that dip in the pond. Trouble was, I could feel her eyes boring into me and I couldn't stand the pressure. Sweat began to pop out on my face, and 'fore I knew it, I spilt the whole story.

When I finished my tale, Eddy threw back her head and laughed, a delightful sparkling sound. "I wish I could have seen that," she said. "Serves them right. Imagine them out carrying on, at their age."

"I'm glad you think it's so funny," I griped. "I'm liable to get in real trouble over the deal."

Eddy laughed again. "Oh, I don't think so," she predicted confidently. "I don't think Iris will say a word. She tries so hard to act prim and stuffy. Do you think she would want the whole town to know she'd been out sparking with Gid? She always lets on like she can't stand him."

"Maybe," I admitted. "But you're forgetting about Gid. All he does is sit in the saloon and gab. Come morning he'll be blabbing the whole story."

"I doubt it. I imagine that Iris will put a muzzle on that mouth of his."

I kicked the ground, thinking it over. Maybe Eddy was right. For the first time I begin to think I might get out of this without getting my tail twisted.

"You hungry?" she asked suddenly. "I think Mother has some stuff left in her basket."

The very mention of food set my mouth to watering and my tongue to wagging. Tying my horse, I started to follow her around to the back, where the party was still going on. Eddy surprised me by dropping back and taking my arm in hers. She kinda leaned her head on my shoulder, and all at once my collar seemed to tighten up.

I moved a finger to run under it, when I realized I didn't even have the top button on my shirt cinched up.

"Don't worry, my mother and father have already gone to the hotel," Eddy said, evidently thinking I was nervous about her father seeing us together—which I sure enough was, after I thought about it.

Swallowing the big lump in my throat, I walked stiffly around to where they had the benches set up against the back wall of the church. As soon as Eddy let go of my arm, I swooped my backside down on one of them benches.

Now that she wasn't hanging onto me, I didn't feel so uncomfortable, but truthfully, I enjoyed her leaning up against me. All of a sudden, my head began to feel woozy. Eddy looked back at me out of the corners of her eyes. Right then, I felt like I'd been kicked in the head, or maybe taken a big snort of that snake juice they keep under the bar at the saloon.

Eddy began to haul the vittles out of that basket and my head started to clear at the sight of them big slabs of roast beef and fresh baked bread. Still, I felt all tense and jumpy inside and every time I looked at her face, it got worse.

Slapping a couple of hunks of beef between two slabs of bread, I tore off a bite, doing my best to look at everything but Eddy. "Looks like this here wingding is starting to die down," I said, feeling the need to say something, anything.

"I suppose it is," Eddy agreed, still pawing through the basket. "If you hurry up and eat, we might have time to dance one more time before they quit playing."

Aw crud, me and my big mouth. "I dunno," I said slowly. Dancing worried me; I was always scared I'd step on the woman or hurt her somehow. Besides, there wasn't anyone dancing. Mostly, the folks were just sitting around shooting the breeze, or singing with the music. I preferred to dance in a crowd where I can kinda hide.

"I don't know if your feet can stand two dances with me, not in one night," I said, hoping to get out of it.

"You only stepped on my foot once last time," Eddy said, holding out a jar of home-canned peaches.

Deciding I was going to have to dance, and figuring it'd go better on a full stomach, I fetched out my hunting knife and speared a slice of peach. Dividing my efforts between them peaches and the sandwich, I done a good job of slicking up that basket.

When I finished eating, I let Eddy drag me out to dance; 'course, by that time, I was starting to get excited about the project. I even managed to clop around for the whole song, and never stepped on her foot once.

As the music died, I walked Eddy back to the benches. For a second, I stood there, mashing my hat in my hands. Eddy placed her hand on my forearm, looking up at me with those shiny black eyes. "Thank you for the dance, Teddy. I really enjoyed it," she said, her voice all soft like.

That wooziness rushed back to my head, and I didn't feel so steady on my feet. I don't reckon I'd ever been this happy.

"Teddy, I was wondering . . . ," Eddy started to say. Maybe she said more, I don't know; I wasn't paying attention.

I saw Betsy walking with Bobby Stamper and got mad all over. They were walking hand in hand, Betsy laughing as Stamper leaned in, whispering something in her ear. A red haze swept across my vision as a terrible fury came on me. Grinding my teeth, I clenched my fists.

"Ouch! Teddy, you're hurting me!" Eddy cried, breaking the hold my anger had on me.

Looking down, I saw I held her hand in my fist. "Sorry about that," I said, rubbing her hand. I felt bad about hurting her hand. She looked like a wounded fawn. "What were you going to ask me?" I asked, trying not to look at Betsy and Stamper. I knew if I looked over there, I'd blow my stack and do something stupid.

"Oh, nothing important," Eddy replied, pulling her hand back. "I best be running along. Pa told us to be at the hotel long before now," she added, sounding distant.

I scratched my head, wondering what in the devil got into her. I could tell she was put out by the stiff way she walked over to Betsy and Stamper.

She spoke briefly to them, then stomped off toward the hotel.

Betsy turned toward Stamper, kissing him. To be polite, I suppose I should have looked away, but I couldn't tear my eyes away from the couple. A hot wave of jealousy surged through me as Betsy broke off the kiss. Their fingers still locked, Betsy backed away. Their hands hung together until their arms would stretch no more. As their hands fell apart, Betsy turned to follow her sister, blowing a kiss back at Stamper. For a second, Stamper stood there frozen, sorta like he was rooted to the spot. Shaking his head, he smiled, sauntering over toward me.

"Lordy, you folks sure know how to throw a shindig," Stamper said, looking like the cat that ate the canary.

I only grunted. I didn't care to talk to Bobby Stamper. What I wanted to do was mash his nose with my knuckles. Still smiling, Stamper didn't even seem to notice my shortness.

"Let's go over to the saloon. I'll buy you a drink," Stamper offered, draping his arm across my shoulders.

Rolling my shoulders, I shed his arm like water off a clay sidehill. Like I said, I was mighty put out with him. "The saloon's likely closed. It's mighty near morning," I said, disgustedly.

"Yes, sir, this was quite a party," Stamper repeated, acting like he never heard me. "Too bad we never got to see that fight you promised me."

"I never promised you no fight," I said, sounding as surly as I felt. "All I said was that Wiesmulluer and Claude generally pitch in and go to fighting every time they see each other. Wasn't my fault that Mrs. Wiesmulluer stopped it this time.

The way she laid the law down, even Turley Simmons couldn't have gotten them going.''

Stamper's hand shot out, grabbing me by the arm and nearly wrenching it from the socket. "What?" he asked, almost snarling. "Are you saying that Turley Simmons is in town?" he demanded to know, all traces of good humor wiped clean from his face.

"Naw, if he had been here, he would have gotten the fight going. Turley always loved deviling those two. He'd make them so mad, they couldn't see straight," I said, watching Stamper relax.

Now maybe I ain't the smartest feller who ever came down the pike, but I was quick enough to notice that anything concerning Turley jerked on Stamper's reins. Why, just mentioning Turley's name was like shoving a handful of bees down Stamper's britches.

But before I had a chance to ask Stamper what was so all fired special about Turley, all tarnation broke loose. First came the scream.

Chapter Four

When I heard that scream, I thought somebody musta squatted on a bear trap. Right on the heels of the scream came the dull boom of a shotgun, blasting once, then again.

For a split second, both me and Stamper stood rooted to the spot, stupefied looks on our faces. "That came from the bank!" Stamper yelled and tore off in that direction.

Lumbering like a foundered cow, I pounded after him. I saw Stamper stop short at the door. It must have been locked, 'cause he went to fussing with the handle.

"Outta the way!" I yelled, lining up on the door.

By now, I'd built up a full head of steam, and when I slammed my two hundred and sixty pounds into that door, something naturally had to give, and it surely did. The whole door ripped loose and skidded across the floor. I caught a glimpse of Andrews sitting on the floor in the back of the bank holding a shotgun.

A glimpse was all I got before I hooked a toe on the doorsill. Losing my balance, I tore across the room, half running and half falling. Before I could regain my balance and get stopped, I smacked into the counter, nailing it head-on. With the sound of snapping and tearing wood the counter tipped over, crashing to the floor.

Shaking the dust from my hair, I sat up in the middle of the ruined counter. Andrews turned his head toward me, his eyes wide as pie plates. He held the shotgun in both hands, the barrels pointed skyward. Piled on top of his head was a mess of plaster and whitewash. Looking up, I saw a jagged hole in the ceiling above his head.

"What happened?" I asked, still trying to get my breath.

"Somebody tried to rob the bank!" Andrews yelled, his voice high and squeaky.

"Is it safe to come in?" Stamper asked, cautiously poking his head inside. He laughed, bending over and slapping his thigh. "Man, when you get started, there ain't no stopping you. I thought you was going to run plumb through the back wall," he said, stepping inside.

"I durn near did," I said, my voice trailing off, as Andrews snapped into action.

"Hold it right there!" he screamed, waving the shotgun in Stamper's direction.

"Whoa," Stamper said, taking a step backward. "What in the devil's got into you?" he asked. He sounded calm, but I noticed he throwed up his hands and grabbed some air.

"You!" Andrews screamed. "I bet you're the one that tried to rob the bank," he said accusingly, the gun shaking in his hands. "But I was too smart for you. I was just waiting for you to make your try,'' the banker said, brandishing the shotgun as he gloated.

"You're crazy," Stamper replied, but he never lowered his hands. I took more than a little satisfaction in noticing that Stamper didn't seem so all fired cocky and blowed up with himself now. 'Course, a scattergun at that range would tend to put a bunch in most folk's drawers.

"Put the gun away, Mr. Andrews," I said tiredly, climbing to my feet.

"I won't do it," Andrews said, setting his jaw firm.

"Aw, shoot, that gun is empty anyway," I said, disgustedly pointing to the hole in the ceiling and its twin in the wall. "Stamper didn't try to rob your bank. He was talking with me when you went to blazing away," I said, wondering why I bothered to stick up for Stamper. I shoulda turned my back and let Andrews blast the smiling devil and get him out of my hair. I was tempted, but like I said, the gun was empty.

"Put it down, Mr. Andrews," I said tiredly.

I'll say one thing for Stamper, he recovered quick. After Andrews lowered the gun, it didn't take Stamper long to slap that smart-alecky smile back on his face.

"What happened?" I asked, taking the weapon from Andrews and stacking it in the corner.

Andrews stabbed a pudgy finger straight at Stamper. "I figured as long as he was in town, I'd better keep an eye on the bank, so I took to sleeping here. Tonight, I heard something outside, so I grabbed my gun." Andrews stopped, looking at the floor and running his tongue over his lips. "I haven't had a lot of experience with firearms; the weapon went off before I was ready." Andrews paused again, still looking down and shifting his feet. ''I didn't even mean to shoot, the gun seemed to go off by itself. It kicked up on me, knocking me down, then it went off again.''

''We heard a scream.'' I prompted.

Andrews looked from me to Stamper, spreading his hands in front of him apologetically. ''I was frightened.''

Already, a crowd of folks had gathered outside, some of them pushing their way inside, all of them shouting and wanting to know what was going on.

''Is our money safe?'' Mr. Claude asked.

His question put a bee in Andrews' bonnet. Wiping the plaster from his face, he stepped up to meet them. ''Don't worry, folks, your money is safe,'' he said hastily. ''There was an attempt on the bank, but as I've always assured you, this bank is thief-proof.'' He shot a dark look at Stamper as the outlaw snorted and rolled his eyes.

The banker cleared his throat, fussing with his collar. ''I might add that the quick and brave action of Mr. Stamper and Sheriff Cooper proved to be instrumental in driving the thieves away. Both men should be praised for their quick action.''

''I'd rather have a beer,'' Stamper said, grinning at the crowd.

''Did the thieves get away?'' Mr. Claude asked.

''I reckon, but as soon as it's light enough to track, I'm going after them,'' I said.

''You better get around. Morning ain't very far away,'' Joe Havens commented, pointing to the sky.

Joe was right. Already, a light glowed in the sky. Morning was almost on us. I frowned, not liking the situation one bit. Looked like I wouldn't get any sleep this night.

"Do you need a posse, Sheriff?" Louis Claude wanted to know.

I shot him a dark scowl and throwed out my chest. "I don't reckon that will be necessary. I can handle this by myself. You folks may as well get on back to bed."

Slowly the crowd drifted away, and as they left I could hear Stamper trying to persuade Joe into opening the saloon. Catching up the lamp from Andrews' desk, I circled around behind the bank. Holding the lamp close to the ground, I squinted, trying to see if there was any tracks.

I'll be danged if I didn't find some. And here I thought ol' Andrews had just been hearing spooks in the night. Stooped over, I hitched along, sorting the trail out.

"You see anything?"

Yeow! I jumped ten feet in the air, dropping the lamp in the process. The lamp smashed to the ground, shattering on impact. Immediately, the flames began to lick at my feet, and believe me, right then I did more dancing than I done all night. Somehow, I managed to stomp the fire out without setting myself ablaze. By the time I finished the job, I was huffing and puffing like a steam train.

"I'm sorry, Teddy, I didn't mean to startle you," Eddy said, trying to cover her laughter with the back of her hand.

"You didn't scare me," I said, putting a hard look on my face. "I just thought everyone had went back to bed. What are you doing here, anyway? You should be in bed."

Eddy's black eyes snapped and she stamped her foot on the ground. "Teddy Cooper, I'll have you know, I'm seventeen years old, and I can do what I please," she said, sticking her nose in the air. "I just came down here to see if you needed anything. I thought if you were going after those men, you might want me to pack you a lunch.''

"Thanks, Eddy, but you needn't bother. I'll get by.''

It's no bother,'' Eddy assured me. Her eyes lowered, looking at the ground. She ran the toe of her shoe in the dust. "Teddy, if you go after those men, be careful.''

"Aw, I'll be fine,'' I scoffed.

"I wouldn't want anything to happen to you,'' she said, her voice so soft that I could barely hear the words.

"Don't worry, I'll be careful,'' I promised, feeling the sudden urge to reach out and touch her.

"Edwina!'' Mr. Wiesmulluer yelled, nearly startling me outta my boots. My hand, which had been reaching out to touch Eddy's cheek, snapped back so quick it almost jerked loose from my body.

Old man Wiesmulluer stood on the street, looking like an avenging angel. Okay, maybe he was dressed only in his red long underwear and floppy boots, but he was still a fearful sight to behold. His long white hair poked out from his head, the whiteness of his hair making his face look even redder and angrier. He wore his pistol belted on over his long underwear and looked of a mind to use it.

"Edwina, get back to the hotel,'' Wiesmulluer thundered, pointing a long gnarled finger in the direction of the hotel.

For someone who was seventeen and old enough to do as she pleased, Eddy sure buttoned her lip and scooted past the old man without so much as a word. Not that I can blame her; that old man could scare the devil himself.

The old man watched her walk away, then turned

his fiery eyes at me. Feeling a shiver, I took a step backward. ''You stay away from her,'' Wiesmulluer threatened, his tone grim as death. ''I won't have a daughter of mine taking up with the likes of you.''

Having spoken his piece, the old man stamped up the street after his daughter. I guess I shoulda been mad at him, but all I could think of was the way Eddy looked, standing there in the moonlight. Just the memory of it made me feel all hot inside and just a little flustered. I don't know how long I stood there with a vision of Eddy's face clouding my eyes, but all of a sudden, I remembered I had a job to do.

Shaking my head, I hurried over to the stable to fetch my horse. Stumbling through the gloom of the barn, I managed to bang my shin on a bucket. Griping at Burdett for not keeping things picked up better, I limped back to the stall where I kept my horse, only to find it empty. Taking off my hat, I scratched my head with both hands. Now what in the devil had happened to my horse?

''Aw, shoot,'' I groaned out loud. I'd left him over by the church. Sometimes I wondered what I used for brains.

Put out at the delay, I hustled over to the church. Sure enough, there he stood munching grass, right where I had left him. Gathering the reins, I led him back down the street.

As I led him past the hotel, Eddy hurried out, carrying a package all bundled up in brown paper. ''Here's something for you to eat,'' she said, shoving the bundle in my arms.

Eddy pressed up against my horse, touching my arm. ''You be careful, Teddy Cooper. I couldn't stand the thought of you getting hurt,'' she said, looking up at me with wide eyes.

For a second, I felt a little misty around the eyes. "I'll come back, just to see you," I said, touching her cheek.

She glanced quickly back at the hotel. "I've got to get back inside. If Pa caught me out here, he'd throttle the both of us."

I didn't move as I watched her hurry to the hotel. At the door she looked back, pressing her fingers to her lips, blowing me a kiss. More than a little embarrassed, I waved back to her, then trudged up the street, a warm, rosy feeling inside me.

By the time I reached the bank, the sun was trying to peek over the rim of the world. Andrews was already busy, doing his best to graft the door back on the front of the bank. After that big buildup he gave me in front of the folks of Whiskey City, he never even looked happy to see me. Looking up from his work, he shot me a dark glance as I led my horse around to the back of the bank.

Dropping the reins, I squatted down, taking a moment to study the tracks. When Andrews cut loose with his scattergun, them men must have taken right out; judging by the way the tracks were scuffed and smeared, they had really been moving too.

Hunkered over like a man with a bad back, I followed the tracks as they led away from town. A couple of hundred yards from town, I found where the men had left their horses. They had milled around some, obviously trying to decide what to do. Here the tracks were clearer, and as I studied them, I decided that there must've been four men. One of them was an awful big man, his tracks cutting into the earth wide and deep.

Frowning, I set my foot beside one of his tracks, resting my weight on that foot. Pulling my foot away, I dropped to my knees. My track and the one of the would-be thief was pretty close to the same. Whoever the man was, he must be about my size, and there weren't many around that big.

Standing up, I looked off in the direction they took. Four in the bunch; one of them about my size. Butch Adkins and his bunch? I wondered. Glancing back toward town, I wished I had taken Mr. Claude up on his offer to round up a posse.

At the time, I hadn't thought that anyone tried to rob the bank. I just figured that Andrews heard something, got scared, and commenced to blasting away. Now that I was faced with the prospect of chasing after four armed and dangerous men, I felt hollow inside.

It came to me that I could go back to town and ask for the posse. I stared back toward town, sorely tempted to do just that. Shifting my feet, I toyed with the reins, wanting to ride back to town and ask for help. After all the bragging I'd done, if I asked for help now, folks might get the idea that I wasn't man enough to handle the job, and I dearly needed this job. I wasn't forgetting that Eddy would be there, and would see me begging for help because I was to scared to go by myself.

Well, that tore it, I was going after those men, and by God I was bringing them back. A feeling of righteous indignation rushing through my veins, I mounted my horse.

I didn't ride far before that feeling begin to play out and nervousness crept up on me. I kept seeing that blonde-haired fella in my mind. If I was any judge, he was the tough one of the litter. I bet that tangling with him would be like getting trapped in a flour barrel with a pair of wildcats.

Licking my lips, I turned in the saddle, looking

back behind me. I shoulda asked Stamper to come with me. Stamper sorta owed me, seeing's how I pulled his fat out of the fire the other day. Anyway, I had the suspicion that it would tickle Stamper pink to see Butch and his crew tossed in the clink. Only thing was, I didn't much care for Mr. Bobby Stamper, and I'd be danged if I would ask him for anything.

Three long hours I followed the trail. I moved along at a good clip, but so had the fellers I chased; that's why their trail was so plain. At the end of the three hours, I couldn't tell that I'd gained any. If anything, I might have lost some ground. I could tell the men were slowing down, and they were starting to take pains to hide their tracks.

My own pace slowed to a bare crawl, as I had trouble staying with the trail. I also kept a watchful eye open for an ambush. It occurred to me that if they feared pursuit, they might drop one man back to slow me down. And a bullet through the brisket would certainly do that job.

At noon, I stopped long enough to gobble down the lunch Eddy packed for me. By now it was a soggy lump of cold meat and bread, but I didn't complain.

That Eddy, she sure was full of surprises. I could picture the way her dark hair fell against her shoulder and the shine in her midnight black eyes. I tried to keep my thoughts away from her; every time I thought of her, my head whirled and I began to get all confused.

Pushing all thoughts of her aside, I licked my fingers and took back after the trail. I walked now, my head down as I followed the dim trail. A couple of hours later, I lost it. The men I followed had crossed a stream, the rushing water wiping out their tracks. I pulled up in the middle of the stream, letting my horse drink while I pondered the situation.

I had no idea which way they went, upstream or down. If they were intent on leaving the country, they would likely head upstream and into the mountains. If they planned to remain in the area and have another go at the bank, they would head downstream, circling around back toward town.

Now, even if I did happen to guess their direction, the chances of picking up their trail once they left the water was slim to none. I wouldn't know for sure which side of the creek they would leave the water, and one thing was certain, they would pick a spot where their tracks would be hard to spot.

Still, it wasn't in me to just give up, so I started downstream, chafing at the slowness of my pace. Even if I were lucky enough to find their trail where they left the stream, I'd be so far behind I wouldn't have a prayer of catching up. I didn't care for the stream either. There was a million places a body could lay in ambush and blow me out of the saddle without even raising a sweat.

Remembering what happened in the saloon, I slipped the thong off my pistol. I rode only a few more yards, then pulled my rifle from the saddle boot, carrying it in my hands. I wanted my weapons ready to use if the need should arise.

I forced myself to stay with the task for several miles, my stomach twisted in knots the whole time. Finally, I gave up.

Touching a spur to my horse, I urged him up the bank, blowing a big sigh of relief when we topped out on flat ground. There ain't much that scares me when I can see it coming, but I don't mind saying that I didn't like it down in that creek, not one bit.

It put a strain on my nerves wondering if an ambusher hid in every shadow or behind every rock and tree.

Lifting my horse into a canter, I took off my hat, letting the wind dry the sweat on my head. Funny that I'd been sweating like that, it had been right cool down in that stream bed.

Slowing my horse back to a walk, I put my hat back on. Yawning, I rubbed my face. The loss of a night's sleep was catching up with me.

Unhooking my canteen from the saddlehorn, I took a long drink, then splashed some water on my face, trying to bring myself back to life. Despite my efforts, it wasn't long before I was dozing in the saddle. Darkness caught me, and I was still a long ways from town. I was, however, close to the Wiesmulluer place. If I had things calculated right, they'd be setting down to supper before long. If I hustled, I could make it there in time to lend them a hand with the eating.

Lights blazed inside their house as I rode into the yard. As I dismounted, old man Wiesmulluer marched out on the porch. He cradled a rifle in his arms, peering into the night. "Who goes there?" he demanded, craning his neck.

"It's me, sir, Ted Cooper," I said, before the old goat decided to ventilate me on general principles.

"Whadda you want?" he asked, sounding about as friendly as a timber wolf.

"I was just passing by and thought maybe I could stop and rest a spell. Maybe even mooch a cup of coffee," I replied, starting to feel a little foolish.

On his own, I reckon the old devil would have

just told me to get, but he never got the chance. His wife came outside, shouldering him aside.

"Teddy, have you been out chasing them outlaws all day?" she asked, and I nodded in return. "My goodness, you must be beat. Come on inside. We were just sitting down to supper, and you are more than welcome to join us."

I don't rightly reckon Wiesmulluer cared for his wife inviting me in. I don't think he liked me much. I didn't take it personal, 'cause I don't think he liked anybody much.

As we trooped inside, the girls were setting the table, both of them looking as pretty as new pennies. Betsy merely glanced at me, but Eddy's face lit up like a desert sunrise.

"Here, Teddy, you can sit by me," Eddy offered, dragging a chair back for me.

Wiesmulluer opened his mouth to say something, but his wife gave him a shove in the direction of the table. "Sit down, dear, we're ready to eat," she said sweetly.

Mr. Wiesmulluer asked us to bow our heads as he said grace. I bowed my head, but I rolled my eyes up, surveying the table while the old man rambled on. What I saw put my mouth to watering and made me wish he'd speed things up. There was a big platter of meat, a bowl of potatoes, and some thick gravy, as well as some fresh baked biscuits. By the time Wiesmulluer finally finished, I was ready to stand up and do a belly flop in the middle of that table, but these folks did things more civilized. They passed everything around the table, taking a small helping as it went by.

It occurred to me that these folks wouldn't fare too well in a bunkhouse full of cowboys. There a body better belly up to the grub and throw a few elbows or else he's liable to go hungry.

"Teddy, did you catch those men that tried to rob the bank?" Eddy asked.

I'd already started eating and had to swallow a big mouthful before I could answer. "No. I trailed them all the way to Buffalo Creek. They went into the water, and I lost the trail. I followed the creek aways, trying to find where they came out, but it wasn't no use."

"Do you think they left the country, or will they be back?" Marie Wiesmulluer asked.

"I don't rightly know. The way I see it, if they were leaving the country, we're well rid of them, and no need of me wasting time hunting them down. If they do plan to take another whack at the bank, then it would be better if I were in town, not out in the hills chasing my tail."

"That's pretty good thinking," Wiesmulluer admitted grudgingly. "I never knew you had that much sense."

I didn't know quite how to take that, so I just concentrated on shoving them groceries down my neck. All this talking was slowing down my eating, but I reckon I was holding my own. I already had my plate slicked up and was ready for another dose.

"Have some more meat," Mrs. Wiesmulluer offered, passing the platter my way.

"Thank you, ma'am," I said, eyeing the platter, sorting out which piece was the biggest. There was two pretty near the same size, so I drug them both off the platter and onto my plate.

"Do you have any idea who those men were?" Eddy asked, passing me the spuds.

I took the bowl from her, giving her a smile of thanks. "I've got a good idea who they were," I answered, and the old man snorted. Shooting him a mean look, I spooned them taters onto my plate.

"Judging from the tracks, there were four men in the group. One of them was a big man, almost as big as me. There ain't many around as big as me, so that narrows it down some," I said, looking at Eddy's sweet face while I talked.

"Humph, there ain't many buffaloes around as big as you," Wiesmulluer fumed. " 'Course, if they ate like you . . . " The old man's voice trailed off, and a grimace shot across his face, so I figured his wife kicked him under the table. You know, I think I liked her.

"You went after four men all by yourself. You must be very brave," Eddy said, a little breathless.

I felt my face growing red. "I guess that's what they pay me for," I sputtered.

"You said you knew who the men were?" Betsy asked, taking an interest in our conversation. I looked across at her and she looked lovely leaning across the table, resting her chin in her hands. "Who were they?"

"Four fellers came in the saloon the other day. They started a ruckus with Stamper. One of them was a big man. They were a salty-looking bunch, and I have an idea they were the ones that tried to rob the bank."

As I talked, I stole a glance over at Eddy. I tell you, sitting here with Betsy and Eddy was nice, but it was also confusing. I didn't know what to think. Two women. Each one special to me. I found myself wishing I was two men.

"Anyway, I put a stop to the scuffling and suggested that they leave," I said, not sure who I was trying to impress.

"Did they leave town?" Eddy asked.

I shrugged, pushing my empty plate away. "They left, but I don't think they went far. I figure they camped close to town, just waiting for a chance to hit the bank."

"You should scout around and find where they camped," Wiesmulluer said, firing up an evil-smelling pipe. "If they decide to come back, they might use the same camp," he added disgustedly, when I looked confused.

Even if I hated to admit it, he had a good point. "Thank you, sir, I'll do just that," I said, forcing myself to be polite. "And thank you, ma'am. I don't know when I ate a better meal." Pushing back my chair, I stood up to leave.

"It's too late to ride all the way into town tonight. You should stay the night here," Eddy said, clutching my sleeve as I rose to leave.

"Edwina is right, Teddy. Why, it'd be almost morning before you reached town. We have a room with a cot in the barn that you are more than welcome to use," Marie Wiesmulluer offered.

"Thank you, ma'am. I am tired. Didn't get any sleep last night," I said, noticing the pleased look on Eddy's face.

"I can show him the room and where to stable his horse," Betsy offered quickly.

Startled, I looked up at her, then glanced over at Eddy, who looked like a lost puppy. For a second, nobody said a word while I wormed in my chair.

"That would be fine, dear. Be sure to get him an extra blanket," Marie said. "Eddy, would you help me with the dishes?"

While Betsy went to fetch my blanket, I helped Mrs. Wiesmulluer and Eddy cart them dishes into the kitchen. I tried to catch Eddy's eye, but she wouldn't look at me. We piled them dishes on a counter while Marie heated water to scrub them in.

"Are you ready, Teddy?" Betsy called from the front door. She stood there, holding the blanket in one hand, the other resting lightly on her hip. Just looking at her was enough to set my heart to racing. I saw the hurt look Eddy gave us, but I done my best to ignore it.

Leading my horse, I followed Betsy down to the barn. "You can put your horse in there," she said, indicating an empty stall. "There's some feed in the manger. While you tend your horse, I'll go fix up your bed."

Since it was summer, they had the big door at the end of the barn open, letting in some moonlight, but it was still a little dark once Betsy left with the lantern. Working by feel, I stripped the saddle from my horse, rubbing him a little.

Betsy sat on the corner of the bed, when I stumbled into the room. Well, it wasn't really a bed, just a pallet fastened to the wall, but I had slept in worse places, so I figured I'd make do.

Betsy stood up in one graceful movement, gliding across the floor, coming to stand next to me. "You must be very brave and strong to go chasing after four desperate men all by yourself," she murmured, placing her hand flat on my chest. I imagine she could feel my heart hammering in my chest. I know it was thumping like a runaway train.

"That's my job," I said, shifting my feet.

"I guess it is," she said softly, pressing her body up against mine. "You know that fellow, Bobby Stamper?"

"Yeah, I know him," I said sourly.

"Do you think you could whip him?"

" 'Course, I could," I said boldly, then I got confused. "I thought you were sweet on him."

Betsy patted her hand on my chest, making a *tisking* sound and rolling her eyes toward the ceiling. "Don't be silly," she said, laughing. "I'd heard of him and wanted to see what he was like. I don't think he is nearly as strong and brave as you," she said, then added after a moment's hesitation, "or as handsome as you either."

Well, let me tell you, I swelled like a bullfrog and felt as big as two men. Before I knew it, Betsy grasped me by the back of the neck, stood up on her toes, and pressed her lips against mine. For a brief wonderful second, we clung together, then she stepped back. She was breathing a little hard, and her face was a mite flushed as she stared at me with a funny glint in her eyes.

"Teddy, what would you do if you were rich?" Betsy asked suddenly.

The question caught me by surprise, and I had to think on it for a minute. "I don't rightly know," I admitted. "It ain't likely to happen."

Betsy gave me a funny smile. "You never know."

"What do you mean?" I asked, scratching my head.

"I heard something, that's all," she said. "I've got to get back up to the house. If Pa caught us, he'd be after you with his shotgun."

She gave me a quick kiss on the cheek, then rushed past me. I listened to her footsteps as she ran all the way up to the house. For a while after she left, I paced the tiny room, my weariness forgotten.

Finally, I undressed and slipped into bed, but it wasn't any use. Despite the long hard day I'd put in and the fact that I hadn't slept the night before, I couldn't drift off. I was all keyed up, and my head whirled with confusing thoughts.

Getting out of bed, I prowled the room like a caged panther. Finally, I reckon I wore myself out, and was able to fall asleep. I didn't wake until I heard Wiesmulluer banging around out in the barn as he went about his morning chores. Jumping out of bed, I dressed in a flash, hurrying out to lend him a hand. I helped him fork hay to the stock and milk their two milk cows.

"I swear, you sleep like you eat," Wiesmulluer grumbled as I handed him a pail of milk from the black-and-white cow. "You always sleep away half the day?"

"No sir. I reckon I was a mite tuckered last night," I answered, pulling my saddle from the fence.

Wiesmulluer leaned against a post, watching while I latched my saddle on my horse's back. "When you get done there, come up to the house. I 'spect they'll have breakfast ready," he said, walking up to the house ahead of me.

I felt a thrill of excitement rush through me. Hustling up, I finished saddling and led my horse up to the house, almost catching up with the old man.

Before Wiesmulluer even opened the door, I could smell the vittles cooking. Edging up close, I peeked eagerly over his shoulder. I could see Mrs. Wiesmulluer and Betsy setting the table, but nowhere did I see Eddy.

A bit disappointed, I followed Wiesmulluer into the kitchen. "Here, Teddy, I saved you a place," Betsy said, motioning for me to sit beside her.

"Where's Eddy?" I asked, trying to sound casual.

"She isn't feeling well this morning," Marie Wiesmulluer answered quietly.

"What's got into her?" Wiesmulluer growled.

"Hush, dear," Marie commanded. "I mean, eat your breakfast," she added in a softer tone.

"Have some eggs, Teddy," Betsy offered as she spooned the scrambled eggs onto my plate.

It'd been a long time since I'd had eggs, but it didn't make up for the fact that I wasn't going to get to see Eddy this morning.

After we ate, I stalled around, hoping she would come down, but I was to be disappointed. Finally, I gave up and said my good-byes.

As I rode out of the Wiesmulluer yard, I looked back and saw Eddy looking out her bedroom window. I waved, but she just turned away, letting the curtain fall.

A heavy feeling settling on me, I rode slowly away.

Darn it, I should be happy. Betsy was finally paying attention to me. Over and over, I kept telling myself that I should be jumping up and down, but I kept picturing Eddy standing at her window, looking so hurt.

As I rode toward Whiskey City, I tried to think of something, anything, to take my mind off Eddy's sad face. I wondered what Betsy had meant with all the business about being rich. And what was all that about me whipping Stamper?

I guess I'm not the smartest guy in the world, 'cause I couldn't figure it out. Little did I know that was the least of my worries. Changes were taking place at this very minute. Events were shaping up that would forever change the lives of everyone in Whiskey City, and not for the better.

Chapter Five

As I rode in, the town didn't look much different than it did on any other day. Maybe a few more horses stood at the hitching rail in front of the saloon, and the front of the bank was still all boarded up, but otherwise things appeared about normal. Certainly, there was nothing to indicate the grief that was about to rain down on us like a horde of locusts.

Yawning, I rubbed my tired eyes, debating whether to go straight to bed or stop by the saloon for a beer first. The bed sounded mighty inviting, but the beer would likely help me sleep. Before I knew it, I up and talked myself into having that beer.

Feeling good about having made a decision, I guided my horse over to the hitching post in front of the saloon. As I tied him to the rail, a huge roar rumbled from inside.

Now what in the world was that all about? Frowning, I stepped on the boardwalk. I stopped, wiped the dust from my badge, and threw my shoulders back. If there was trouble in there, I'd darn sure put a stop to it. A serious expression riding on my face, I went in. A gust of laughter greeted my ears as I pushed through the swinging doors.

A tremendous cloud of smoke billowing over their heads, a group of men stood crowded at the bar. It looked like half the men in the county must be in here today. "What's going on?" I asked, the smoke stinging my eyes.

Joe Havens looked up from behind the bar. "Howdy, Sheriff!" he yelled, giving me a big wave. "You catch your bank robbers?" he asked, laughing gleefully.

Joe's face was flushed beet red and from the way he swayed on his feet. I'd say that he'd sampled about as much whiskey as he served. Fact is, every man in the place looked like they'd been lapping up Joe's firewater.

"No, I didn't catch them. I lost the trail at Buffalo Creek," I said, stepping up to the bar.

Rocking on his feet, Mr. Andrews flopped his meaty arm across my shoulders. "That is a shame, son, but I'm sure you done your best."

I had to lean in close to catch what he was mumbling and even then I had a hard time understanding him. Part of it was because his lower lip was sagging almost down to his belt. As the banker's words trailed off, his head tipped forward, and I thought he was going to fall asleep. All of a sudden, his head snapped back up and he let out a bellow that dang near deafened me. "Joe! Fetch our good sheriff a drink."

Joe nodded, his head bobbing up and down like a pump handle. He turned to get me a glass, knocking off several before he got his paws wrapped around one. He plopped the glass on the bar upside down and tried to fill it twice before I turned it over for him.

Grinning crookedly, Joe stared at the glass. "Darn thing was upside down. Now who in the heck done that?" he mumbled, splashing the glass full.

"What are you boys celebrating?" I asked, doing my best to ignore that glass. I've noticed that 'bout the only thing Joe's whiskey is good for is cleaning your rifle. 'Course, you have to be careful, or it will eat all the blue off the barrel. Me, I try to avoid the stuff every chance I get.

"We are drinking a toast to our good friend, Turley Simmons!" Louis Claude said, his French accent coming through loud and clear. "Here's to Turley!"

With Mister Claude's words, every man in the place let out a howl and downed their drinks. Since everyone took a snort, it didn't seem polite for me not to partake, so I slurped down part of my drink.

"Where is Turley?" I asked, looking for him and listening for his cackling laughter.

"Turley's dead," Mr. Andrews said, his slurred voice sounding sad. "Here's to Turley!"

"What . . . ?" my words were drowned as a cheer went up for Turley and everyone had another drink. I went along with them, gagging a mite on mine. "What happened to Turley?" I managed to croak.

"Unfortunately, his heart gave out," a quiet voice said.

Peering through the smoke, I saw a smallish man in a fancy suit sitting at a table in the back. As I watched, he stood up, walking toward me. He held a drink in his hand, but from the look of him, I don't think he had been drinking, Least ways, not nearly as much as these other fellers.

"Phillip Bartholomew Thomas, attorney at law," he said, offering his hand. "All of this," he said, sweeping the bar with a wide gesture, "was Mr. Simmons's last wish."

"And a darn fine idea it was! Here's to good ol' Turley!" Gid Stevens roared, and another toast was drunk.

Thomas didn't drink. He merely watched the proceedings with an air of distaste. "Mr. Simmons wished the good men of Whiskey City to drink a toast to his memory, then hear the reading of his will." Thomas wrinkled up his nose as his glance traveled the room. "I think we can safely assume that we've covered the toast and can now move on to the reading of the will."

With a flourish, Phillip Thomas pulled a paper from beneath his coat. "This is the last will and testament of Tiberius Barneby Simmons."

Thomas fished a pair of flimsy spectacles from his coat pocket and slipped them on. "I, Turley Simmons, leave all my money to my wife, Lilly. I don't know rightly how much money I have, but it's a pretty fair pile and should last Lilly the rest of her days."

Thomas looked over the top of the paper, his eyes taking us all in as we waited breathlessly for him to go on. "This is the part that concerns you men," he said.

"To the good folks of Whiskey City who have always treated me right and made me feel at home, I leave my gold mine!"

As Thomas's voice died away, dead silence settled on the barroom. The silence was shattered as

Andrews's drink slipped through his fingers, smashing on the floor. "Gold mine," Andrews whispered, his voice reverent. "Gawd almighty! Did you really say gold mine?"

"Yes, gold mine," Thomas repeated, then continued his reading. "The mine belongs to whoever finds it. I hid a map which tells the location of the mine. You folks can look for the mine or the map, but I'm warning you, I hid the map real good. It's in the safest place I could think of."

Thomas took off his glasses, folded them, and placed them carefully in his pocket. "There you have it, gentlemen. The mine belongs to the person who locates it. I wish you all luck."

For a second, nobody said a word, the whole bunch of us plumb stumped. "Yippee!" Burdett yelled, giving us all a start. "We're gonna be rich!" he yelled, holding his glass high and dancing around the room.

"Wait a minute. Hold your horses!" I shouted, holding my hand up. "You believe Turley had a gold mine? Shoot, he was always broke," I said, my words sure cutting the party short. I reckon everyone recalled the way Turley was always spooning a free drink or mooching a dollar. A growl traveled through the crowd as they realized what I said was true.

"Mr. Simmons left his wife a considerable estate. Several thousand dollars," Thomas said.

"So old Turley was a rich man. Who'd ever thought that?" Gid asked, rubbing his chin. " 'Course, who'd ever thought he had a wife?"

"Can you imagine what kind of a woman it would take to put up with Turley?" Joe Havens asked, and judging from the blank looks, I don't reckon they could.

"Never mind that," Andrews said, shoving Mr. Burdett out of the way to get to Thomas. "Tell us more about the mine. Did Turley say anything about where he might have hidden the map?"

"Yeah, come on Phil, tell us what he said," Gid Stevens urged, draping his arm across Thomas's shoulders.

"It's Phillip," Thomas replied curtly, and not so gently removed Gid's arm.

"What about the mine? Did Turley tell you anything?" Andrews asked, his voice almost pleading.

Thomas shrugged his thin shoulders. "Mr. Simmons did not confide in me. All he did say was that there was more gold in that mine than a man could spend in ten lifetimes. Millions of dollars."

Andrews made a gurgling sound in his throat as he clutched the bar. He grabbed a glass and sucked down a long drink. "Did you say millions?" he asked, his voice a bit raw.

"That's what I said," Thomas replied curtly. His business completed, Thomas downed his drink, placing the glass on the bar. "Good day, gentlemen," he said, and marched stiff backed from the room.

As soon as Thomas left, bedlam broke out. You never seen so much whooping and hollering in your life. As soon as they got that out of their systems, the men of Whiskey City went to plotting and planning. They argued back and forth about where the mine could be and where Turley might have hidden the map. In between, they managed to put away a lot of Joe's whiskey.

Stamper didn't join in the fun; instead he slunk over to a table. For once, he wasn't grinning and just plain looking happier than a man had a right to be. A glass and full bottle sat on the table in front of him, but Stamper wasn't drinking. Taking my own glass, I crossed over to his table.

"Well, I reckon the cat is out of the bag now," Stamper said, picking up his glass and staring into its contents.

"Huh?" I blurted out, not picking up on what he meant.

In one quick, almost angry motion, Stamper raised the glass to his lips, tossing the whiskey down his throat. "Turley's gold mine! Everybody in town knows about it now!" Stamper said, slamming the empty glass down on the table.

"The gold mine! That's why you are in town. You never meant to rob our bank at all," I sputtered, wondering if the gold mine was what Betsy had been talking about the other night. I figured it most likely was. Somehow she'd wormed the story out of Stamper. More'n likely he'd been bragging, trying to impress her.

Stamper smiled tiredly. "Well, I did have an idea the map might be in the bank."

"How come you didn't just crack open that safe and see?"

Stamper sighed, rubbing his forehead like he had a headache. "Mainly because, if the map wasn't there, I'd be in trouble. You knew who I was, and if the bank got robbed, I'd either be in jail or running out of the country."

"You shouldn't have told us your real name," I commented, taking a small sip.

"I never intended to," Stamper said, "but then Butch showed up, calling me by name, so I had very little choice."

"You reckon Butch and his men are here for the gold?"

"I 'spect so," Stamper said, looking none too happy about it. "They was in Kansas City the same time me and Turley was, and you know Turley. Him trying to keep a secret is like trying to dam a river with a screen door."

I nodded my head; that was sure enough true, Turley could talk the leg off a sawhorse. "How'd you happen to find out about the mine?"

Stamper shrugged, filling both our glasses. "I was loafing around in Kansas City, and one night I got into a poker game with Turley and some other men. After the game broke up, me and Turley sat around all night just drinking and shooting the bull. He got to bragging about this gold mine he had near Whiskey City."

Stamper took a sip of his whiskey. "Now, mind you, I had my doubts. I've known Turley off and on for a long time, and he never acted like he had money, but then I got to thinking. Turley lost a pile of money in the poker game that night and he never acted like it bothered him. I figured if anyone would find gold in them mountains, it would be Turley. He's wandered them all his life."

"How'd you find out about the map?" I asked, leaning forward.

"When I showed interest in the mine, Turley clammed up, so I made the remark that a body could find gold up in them hills, then not be able to find it when he went back."

Stamper laughed, shaking his head. "Turley bulled up, allowing as to how he made a map and stashed it in a real safe place. That's all he would say about the gold; we got to talking about other things. Turley told me about this safe in Whiskey City that nobody could open. Turley didn't know what kind it was, but I figured it had to be a Harper-Evans.''

''And you figured he had the map stashed in the bank's safe? That don't make sense to me. If the map was in the safe, why would he even mention the safe?''

''Maybe he wanted me to think the map was in this uncrackable safe so I wouldn't bother coming to look for it,'' Stamper said, shrugging.

''Aw shoot, the map ain't in the safe,'' I said, taking a drink. ''If it were, Andrews would know about it. He'd be halfway up to the mine by now.'' I looked over to make sure Andrews hadn't left, but he still stood, propped up against the bar.

''He might not know. Maybe Turley gave him some papers to put in the safe for safekeeping. He wouldn't know there was a map to a gold mine in amongst them,'' Stamper reasoned.

''He'd know now,'' I said, shaking my head. ''You can bet if Turley ever left any papers with Andrews, that old skinflint would be pawing through them right now.''

''You might be right about that,'' Stamper said, toying with the bottle. ''The only thing I know for certain is that whoever finds that map is going to be a rich man.''

That might be true, but right then a gold mine didn't interest me near as much as the bed waiting on me over at the hotel. Pushing back my chair, I said good night to Stamper.

The party at the bar was losing steam fast. There wasn't any dancing around now. Mostly, they were hanging onto the bar, telling stories about Turley.

''Remember the time Turley put a dose of salts in the whiskey?'' Joe Havens asked, laughing at the memory.

"Yeah, then he nailed the door shut on the outhouse," Burdett said, roaring with laughter.

Claude leaned against the bar, his chin resting on its smooth top. "Good ol' Turley. I miss him already," he said in a woeful tone and wiped a tear from his eye.

As I walked out, I heard them recounting Turley's exploits. One thing about Turley, he loved nothing better than a good joke on somebody.

The next morning, I awoke with my tongue feeling fuzzy as a wool blanket. Rubbing the sleep from my eyes, I yawned. Then, taking my time, I got dressed and left my room.

Whiskey City looked like a ghost town when I stepped out on the street. Not a soul stirred, but I guess they were still sleeping it off.

As I looked down the empty street, Stamper stepped out of the hotel beside me. Stamper didn't look so good this morning. Fact is, he looked miserable as an elephant with a runny nose.

"I figured everybody would be out looking for Turley's mine this morning," Stamper said.

"Give 'em time. By noon, they'll all be in a fret to find the mine," I predicted.

"A man would be crazy to look for the mine without the map. Them mountains cover a lot of territory," Stamper said.

"Maybe so, but how about the map? Turley could have hidden it anywhere."

"That's right," Stamper agreed sourly. "What we got to figure out is where. You got any ideas?"

"I figured you might know," I commented slyly. "You shoulda known him pretty well, him being your uncle and all."

For just a second, Stamper's flashing grin was

back. "Did I say that?" he asked, looking at the sky and sounding mighty innocent.

"I seem to recall you saying something along those lines," I replied, sharing his light mood. "If I know Turley, he hid that map in a good place. The last place in the world anyone would ever think to look."

"And where would that be?" Stamper asked, his voice straining to be casual.

I laughed, shaking my head. "Now that's a mighty good question, and if I knew the answer, I'd go get the map for myself."

"You mean to say that you wouldn't share with your good buddy Bobby Stamper?" he asked, giving me a cheesy grin.

"Sheriff! Sheriff, come quick!" young Roger Burdett screamed, tearing up the street like a prairie twister.

"Whoa. Hold up there, boy," I said, grabbing the lad by the collar to keep him from skidding past us. "What's your big toot?"

Roger's little, round face was redder'n a tomato. He had to take a couple of deep breaths and wipe his nose on his sleeve before he managed to spit out his story. "There's a big ruckus down at Mister Turley's old dugout. Pa sent me to fetch you. He said come quick 'fore someone gets killed!"

I looked over at Stamper, who stared back open-mouthed. "They found the map!" we screamed together, and took off.

By the time I covered a block, Stamper had a good lead on me. Pumping my arms, I tried to run faster, but speed isn't one of the things I'm built for. I mean, I could likely run down a three-legged turtle, providing of course that he didn't have much of a head start, but that's about the size of my running abilities.

Ahead of me, Stamper rounded the corner at the end of the street at a dead run. The old dugout was built into a mound about a hundred yards behind Burdett's barn. I'd seen that dugout a hundred times, but never knew it belonged to Turley.

Huffing and puffing, I lumbered around the corner, plowing right over Stamper, who for some dang fool reason decided to stop. We crashed to the ground in a tangled mess, both of us cussin' like muleskinners.

Kicking free of Stamper, I lunged to my feet. I started to take off again, then stopped cold in my tracks, not believing what I saw.

Chapter Six

Never in all my born days did I ever see such a sight. Most of the town had gathered at that dugout, and believe me, they weren't having no box social neither. A brawl raged down there that made the whole Civil War look like a little scuffle between schoolboys.

Gid Stevens had Harvey Case, who worked for Claude, around the neck. While Gid held Harvey, Iris battered him with her purse. Apparently, Iris wasn't satisfied with the results she was getting, 'cause she threw down that purse and snatched up a handy piece of driftwood.

Iris sighted in for a second, then hauled back like a man throwing a cowchip. "Take this, you dirty polecat!" she yelled and cut loose with a mighty swipe.

The trouble was that Harvey twisted away from Gid and managed to duck. Gid wasn't so lucky.

That piece of driftwood smacked him right on the ear. Bawling like a lost calf, Gid flipped over backward.

Iris sure never let Gid's plight bother her any. She just took another cut at Harvey. Holding his hat on with one hand, Harvey used his other hand and tried to fend off Iris's attack while he looked desperately for a place to hide.

While Iris pummeled Harvey, Joe Havens and Mr. Burdett crashed out through the flimsy door, locked in mortal combat. They hit the ground, rolling around, biting and carrying on like you wouldn't believe.

Andrews poked his head out, a greasy smile smacked all over his face. He looked both ways, then came pussyfootin' through the door, clutching a chunk of stovepipe. He stepped daintily over Joe and Burdett as they battled, then scurried toward town. He never made it.

Like a Comanche warrior, Claude charged out of the cabin, screaming a bunch of high-pitched French words. Now, I ain't right certain what them words meant, but I'd guess they was cuss words.

Either way, Claude barreled full tilt into Andrews. Grunting like a pig, Andrews spilled over, hitting the ground hard. Andrews lost his grip on that hunk of stovepipe, and it rolled across the ground. Both Andrews and Claude took after that pipe, doing their best to elbow the other out of the way.

Right about then, I decided I'd best do something before them folks killed each other. Waving my arms over my head and ordering them to stop, I charged down toward the melee. Them folks, they never paid no more attention to me than a big bird. Gid Stevens got to his feet and pitched in to help Iris. Together, they gave Harvey a right good mauling. I tried to bull in and stop them and almost lost my nose as Iris drawed back her club. Grabbing the club as it went back by, I wrenched it from Iris's hands.

A pistol shot sounded, followed by two more quick ones. With the sound of them shots, the brawl came to a ragged, stumbling halt. The whole bunch turned to see what all the gunplay was about.

Every eye turned to see Bobby Stamper holding his pistol over his head, a trickle of smoke rising lazily from the business end of that hogleg. "I believe the sheriff has something to say," Stamper said mildly as he slipped the gun back into his holster.

Darn tootin' I had something to say, all right. I just didn't know what. Clearing my throat a couple of times, I let my eyes roam the mess of folks in front of me.

"What the Sam Hill is going on here?" I roared. "Have you folks been chewing on loco weed?"

"Now Sheriff, you got no call to scream at us," Iris Winkler said through tight lips. "Me and Gid, we came up with the idea to search this place first. Then these other yahoos came over and started trying to horn in," she added, her seething gaze traveling over the crowd.

"That's right, Sheriff. If the map is here, it rightfully belongs to Iris and myself," Gid put in.

But I didn't pay him no mind. I just stared openmouthed at the collection of folks still pouring out of the dugout.

"Well, Sheriff, are you going to throw these people off this place or not?" Iris demanded.

"I don't know who was here first, but it seems to me that if the map is here, everybody should split the mine," I said, awful proud of myself for hitting on the perfect solution. If I was proud of my idea, no one else was. The roar of protest that rained down on my ears was both loud and immediate.

Andrews climbed to his feet, still clutching that piece of pipe. "See here, Sheriff, I'm the one that thought to look in the stove and whatever is in this pipe belongs to me!"

"Aw, go sit on a pasture muffin. I was just fixin' to have a gander at that stove when you shoved your snout in!" Joe Havens declared hotly.

Andrews didn't bother wasting any words, he simply slapped that stovepipe over Joe's head. When he clobbered Joe, a big ball of soot shot out of the pipe, splattering Iris full in the face.

In a heartbeat, it got quiet as death. While Joe staggered in a wobbly manner, Iris stood there blinking and sputtering. Now, I don't know if it was soot blowing off her face, or if smoke was actually coming out of her ears, but I do know that ol' gal was on the prod. If looks could kill, the terrible one she shot at Andrews woulda put the rest of us to digging an extra wide hole to plant the chubby sucker in.

Mumbling under his breath, Gid Stevens went to rolling up his sleeves, muttering something about defending Iris's honor. Most times, I might have enjoyed watching them two old duffers battle, but this morning, I was plumb out of patience.

I snagged both of them by the backs of their collars and shook them a mite. "What I said before goes. It's share and share alike, and that goes for whatever is in that pipe.'' Not bothering to be gentle, I set Andrews and Gid back on the ground. ''Mr. Andrews, I'd appreciate it if you would fish out whatever is in that pipe.''

I don't guess the banker liked me telling him what to do, but the treasure bug had got ahold of him. Dropping to his knees, he felt inside the pipe. As one mass, the folks crowded in close, holding their breath.

Bobby Stamper made the mistake of trying to edge past Blanche Caster. Let me tell you, this wasn't the same sweet old woman who used to bake molasses cookies and bring them to us kids at the school. There dang sure wasn't anything sweet about the way she shoved Stamper back. ''Mind your manners, sonny,'' she ordered and promptly stomped his toe with the heel of her lace-up shoe.

Stamper managed to bite off most of the howl that threatened to get past his lips, but he done some muttering under his breath. I noticed he stayed back, content to peer over her shoulder now.

''I found something!'' Andrews yelled, slowly pulling his arm from the pipe. ''It feels like a piece of leather.''

You could hear breaths being sucked in and held as the crowd waited. With a little flourish, Andrews yanked a piece of rolled-up buckskin from the stovepipe.

''For God's sake, hurry up,'' Burdett urged, dancing around like he had to go to the outhouse.

''These knots are tight,'' Andrews complained, struggling with rawhide string tied around the skin.

Immediately, a half-dozen hunting knifes were

extended to him, mine among the bunch. Well, I guess I'd went and caught the gold fever myself.

Andrews took Claude's knife and sliced right through the rawhide. Tossing the knife aside, Andrews placed the skin on the ground and began unrolling it. "There's writing on it!" he yelled.

Before he even had it completely unrolled, every eye in the bunch was reading. After everyone finished reading, the silence was so absolute that you could hear the grass growing.

Suddenly, Mr. Burdett exploded. Swearing bitterly, he kicked a rock across the yard.

"*Mon Dieu!*" Mr. Claude exclaimed with a hiss. "I wish Turley was alive and here right now," he said.

"Why's that?" Stamper asked, looking pleased. Believe me, his was the only face in the crowd that looked pleased.

"Because I want to kill him!" Claude said, smacking his fist into his palm.

I reckon if we'd put 'er to a vote, that idea woulda passed hands down. Them folks were hopping mad. They called Turley every name in the book, and a few that weren't in no book.

Andrews still knelt on the ground, staring blindly at the piece of buckskin with a stupefied look on his face. He kept mumbling the words printed boldly on the skin. "Ha, fooled you. You're gonna have to look harder."

Gid Stevens picked up the pipe, holding it up to his face as he squinted inside it. He peered through it twice, and was fixing to look again when Iris slapped it from his hands. "Put that filthy thing down and let's go," Iris snapped, grabbing Gid by the arm and pulling him along.

They made a strange-looking pair as they hustled back to town. The only place on Iris's face that wasn't covered with black soot was around her eyes, and Gid was her opposite with big black rings around his eyes. Iris may have been put out, but I noticed before they were a quarter of the way to town that they had their heads together, whispering back and forth.

"Appears that folks ain't at all pleased with good ol' Uncle Turley," Stamper commented.

"I notice you don't seem awfully upset that the map wasn't here."

"I'm not," Stamper said, shrugging as he rolled a smoke. "A lot of folks here. I'd hate to have to share with all of them."

"You're a generous man," I said, with a touch of sarcasm. Turning my back on Stamper, I went inside so I could keep an eye on things while they finished searching the dugout.

"What's up with Iris and Gid? They seem awfully chummy all of a sudden," Joe Havens said, rubbing his head as Burdett snorted.

"You don't suppose there is anything going on between them?" Claude wondered, looking curiously at Havens and Burdett, who glared fiercely at each other.

"I think they are sparking each other," I said.

Joe laughed harshly, kicking the dirt floor. "How would you know?" he jeered.

"Leave Teddy alone," Burdett said, and promptly shoved Joe into the wall. Joe hit the wall and then fell as a raft of pots and pans tumbled off the wall, clobbering him on the head.

Joe came off the floor cussing and throwing wild punches. Mr. Claude and I jumped in and pulled the two apart. They backed away snarling and snapping like two wild dogs.

The folks had returned to their poking and prying, so I stood back in the corner and let them have at it. Even though their hearts weren't in the task anymore, they searched the place from top to bottom. But they didn't find no map.

I waited as the last of them left, every one of them swearing under their breath and damning the memory of Turley Simmons. After they were gone, I started picking up and straightening the place. I don't know why I bothered, but it didn't seem right to leave everything strewn about on the floor.

I worked an hour or so, then moseyed back to town. I walked slow, and I guess I was daydreaming. My mind was occupied with the thought of all that gold and what I could do with it. I didn't know the stage was even in the country until I heard the driver yell. At the time, I never realized that I was walking down the middle of the street. I glanced back to see the stage bearing down on me. I could see the driver standing up in his seat, sawing back on the reins.

Well, believe me, the sight of those lathered-up horses careening down the street right for me put my big feet to moving. I left the ground in a reckless headlong dive for the safety of the boardwalk. I made it, but just barely, and I lost some hide in the process.

Climbing to my feet, I saw the stage lurch to a halt in front of the hotel, then disappear in the cloud of dust that chased the stage.

I was picking splinters out of my hand with my teeth when I first saw her. She stepped daintily from the stage, holding her skirt outta the dirt with one hand. I was watching her so hard that I clean forgot what I was doing and dang near gnawed one of my fingers off thinking it was a splinter.

Yelping more in surprise than pain, I jerked my fingers out of my mouth, then hid them behind my back as I realized she was coming up to me. She stopped smack-dab in front of me, looking me up and down with a pair of the most beautiful green eyes I ever did see. "I take it that you are the law in this town?"

"Yes, ma'am, I sure enough am," I replied, wondering how she knew that, but then I guessed that she could just tell from looking at me. More'n likely it was the steely glint in my eyes that gave me away. "How'd you know I'm a lawman?" I asked, snatching my hat from my head, along with some hair.

She gave me a quick smile, tapping my badge with a painted fingernail. "You're the one wearing the badge."

Feeling like a fool, I felt my face burn red, which made me feel even worse. To top it off, I couldn't think of a durn thing to say, and believe me, I was trying real hard. All I could do was stare at the ground and scuff my toe in the dirt.

"My name is Lilly Simmons," she said, holding out her hand.

I gotta say, she had a right pretty hand. Long, dainty fingers and some lacy white gloves with no fingers in them. Yes sir, it was a mighty pretty hand, but she never knew the first thing about shaking hands. Not the way she was holding her hand, bent at the wrist, fingers pointing straight down.

It was a mite awkward, but I managed to shake her hand, being real careful not to squeeze too hard, lest I crush her hand. When I released her hand, I saw that fancy white glove wasn't so white anymore. Fact is, the darn thing was almost black.

My jaw sagging, I stared stupidly down at my own hands, which were filthy from all the work I done out at Turley's.

"Aw, crud," I moaned. "I'm real sorry bout that, ma'am. Here, let me wipe that off for you," I added hurriedly.

Licking my thumb, I commenced to rubbing that glove. Right away, I could see I wasn't doing no good, but I kept at it stubbornly, hoping to make things right somehow.

"It's okay, Sheriff," Lilly said, which I thought was right kind of her.

"I think some of it's a-comin' off," I protested, rubbing like crazy.

"I said it was fine," Lilly said, jerking her hand away from mine.

When she jerked back, it caught me off guard. I couldn't get my hand unlatched from hers quick enough, and I brushed against her dress, leaving a black smudge. And this weren't no ordinary dress either. No sir, it was creamy white with more ruffles and frills than a basket of petticoats.

I started to brush away the smudge, then stopped, knowing I'd make it worse. So I didn't do anything, except a lot of stammering and yammering.

Wringing my hands, I shifted from one foot to the other, feeling like a complete fool. "Don't worry, Sheriff, this is an old dress anyway," Lilly said, smiling as she touched my arm. "The reason I wished to speak to you is that my husband owned a mine in this area. I believe you knew my husband, Turley Simmons?"

Well, that nearly floored me. When I heard Turley had a wife, I pictured . . . well, I don't rightly know what I pictured, but it wasn't nothing like the graceful lady standing before me.

"Theodore Cooper!" Eddy Wiesmulluer said, startling me out of my stupor. "My father wants to see you."

"What's he want?" I asked, looking over my shoulder at her. One glance was all I needed to see that Eddy was mad about something. She stood with her feet spread and hands on hips, her lips shut tight.

"Somebody butchered one of our steers. Pa wants you to come out and take a look," she said through clenched teeth.

Now, what in the world was she so all fired mad about? I scratched my head wondering, but then I figured that Eddy seen me ruin Lilly's gloves and fancy dress. "Eddy, this is Lilly Simmons, Turley's widow," I said, remembering my manners.

Eddy didn't act too thrilled to meet Lilly, but I reckon Eddy was still mad at me. She looked Lilly coolly up and down, then turned back to me. "Pa said you was supposed to come out today, or no later than first thing in the morning," Eddy said. She gave Lilly one last look, then flounced away.

"A very pretty young lady. Is she your girl?" Lilly asked, with a knowing look on her face.

Jamming my hands down in my pockets, I shuffled my feet. "Aw, I don't know. She is right pretty and I like her a lot," I mumbled, my face hot.

"I think she must like you," Lilly said, watching as Eddy went in the store. "Your name is Theodore, then?" she asked, looking back at me.

I groaned; I dearly hated Theodore. "That's my name, but I don't like it much," I admitted. "Only time anyone ever calls me Theodore is when I'm in trouble."

"Okay, how about Ted?" Lilly asked, laughing gayly.

"That's what I prefer, but most folks call me Teddy." Lilly's face turned serious. "You're right, Ted sounds much better for a man in a position of authority, such as yourself," she said gravely.

Lilly took my arm, leading me in the direction of the hotel. Seeing stars in front of my eyes, I bumbled along beside her. "I do have some business that I need to discuss with you, but after that terrible ride, I want to freshen up and get some rest first."

We stopped in front of the hotel, Lilly releasing my arm. "How about if I meet you for dinner this evening?"

"That'd be just fine, I reckon." Scratching my head, I watched her breeze into the hotel. Now, what did she mean, she'd meet me this evening for dinner? According to my calculations, it was dinnertime now.

The stage driver came out of the hotel, carrying a sack of mail for the return trip. "Criminy, that woman sure was a looker!" he said, then gave me a sly smile. "Looked like she was taking a shine to you."

"She said she wanted to eat dinner with me, but she wanted to wait until tonight. It's noontime now. I don't reckon I can wait until tonight," I said, following Joe over to the stage.

Joe tossed the mail sack up on the stage, then turned to grin at me. "Shoot, Teddy, that's just the way them fancy-pants eastern folks talk. They don't eat supper like normal folks; they call supper dinner," he explained, putting his arm on my shoulder as we walked around behind the stage.

"You mean they eat dinner twice?"

"Yeah, I reckon. I guess they just don't know any better." The driver shook the stage door, making sure it was shut good, then climbed up in the box. "See you next trip, Teddy," he called, then snapped his whip.

Coughing, I ducked my head, waiting for the dust kicked up by the stage leaving to settle. I wondered if I should ride out to Wiesmulluer's today or wait until morning. If I left now, it'd be late when I got back. I'd promised to meet Lilly to talk law business this evening, so I would have to wait until morning to ride out to Wiesmulluer's. I blew out a big sigh. this law stuff was turning into real work. Seemed like somebody always had something they wanted done.

Out of the corner of my eye, I saw Eddy come out of the store, toting an armload of packages. Hustling, I caught up with her. "Here, let me carry that stuff for you," I offered.

"I can manage," Eddy said shortly.

"Aw, Eddy, don't be mad. I didn't mean to get Lilly's dress all dirty," I said, reaching out and taking the stuff from her arms.

Eddy stepped in front of me, folding her arms across her chest. "I don't give two hoots or a holler about that overgrown dustmop!"

I leaned back, surprised at the fire snapping in her black eyes. "What are you mad about then?" I asked, a little wary of the answer.

"If you don't know, I'm certainly not going to tell you!"

"Eddy, I don't know what I done, but believe me, I'm real sorry," I pleaded, wanting her to forgive me.

Eddy looked at me for a long second, then spun around, walking fast toward her horse. Having a heck of a time balancing them packages in my arms, I hurried after her. "Honest, Eddy, I'm real sorry. I don't want you to be mad at me. That's why I came by your house the other day, just to see you."

Eddy stopped beside her horse, and for a second her face softened. I think she was going to forgive me. Then I had to go and open my big mouth. "Tell your pa I'll be out at your place first thing in the morning. I can't come today, I promised to meet with Miss Lilly. She has some law business to talk over with me."

Boy, let me tell you, that didn't sit well with Eddy. She went to grabbing them packages outta my arms and slamming them in her saddlebags.

"Don't worry. I'll be out at your place first thing. I promise," I said, thinking she was mad because I was putting her pa's problems off.

If I hoped that my promise would make her happy again, I was in for a foolin'. She jerked them bags closed and jumped on her horse without so much as a word. Shooting me a withering look, she jerked her horse's head around, giving him a dose of her spurs.

Feeling miserable, I trudged back down to the hotel. I swear, I don't know what had gotten into Eddy, and just when I was starting to like her.

The lobby of the hotel was deserted, which wasn't unusual for this hour of the day, but I was some surprised to find the kitchen empty. A big pot of beans sat simmering on the stove. On the counter beside the stove was a stack of bowls and spoons, along with a little sign. The sign said beans were two bits and leave your money on the table.

Dropping my money on the counter, I snagged onto a bowl, dishing it full of beans. Grabbing a spoon, I carried my bowl to a table. While I ate, my mind kept stewing over the fact that Eddy was upset with me. I kept trying to come up with something I could do to land myself back in her good graces.

Before I knew, I'd ate that whole bowl of beans and never came up with any answers. Carrying the bowl, I shuffled back over to the stove. Dipping the bowl full again, I wondered if I was supposed to pay again. The sign never said anything about how many bowls a feller could have; it just said beans were two bits. I decided that meant as many beans as a man could hold. Still, I looked both ways to make sure nobody was watching before I hustled back over to my table.

As soon as I sat back down, my mind went to worrying over Eddy again. I couldn't think of anything special I could do for her, but I made up my mind that come what may, I'd be at her pa's ranch come first light.

I swear, worrying over her dang near ruined my dinner. I mean, I ate five bowls, but I never enjoyed them like I shoulda.

Loosening my belt a notch, I tossed my empty bowl on the counter. Strolling through the lobby, I wondered what I was going to do to pass the afternoon. I wanted to take a nap, but didn't dare. If old man Wiesmulluer ever found out I took a snooze instead of hustling out to his place, he'd have my hide. That cantankerous old coot would never understand that there just wasn't time for me to go out to his place, then get back in time to meet Lilly.

I didn't see the call to get all excited over one butchered steer. A hundred to one it was Claude. Every so often, Claude would slaughter one of

Wiesmulluer's steers. Now, that's not to say that Wiesmulluer didn't get even, 'cause he did. He'd raid Claude's melon patch and snap some roasting ears out of the little Frenchman's cornfield.

Dismissing that nonsense from my mind, I headed over to the jail. I wanted to go through the Wanted posters and see if I had anything on Butch Adkins and his bunch. I had a feeling we hadn't seen the last of them varmints.

The Wanted posters were piled carelessly in the bottom drawer of the desk. Tossing my hat on the desk, I pulled them out and started poring through them. Vance Sellers, who'd been sheriff before me, hadn't been very organized, and the posters weren't in any kind of order. Reading through them, it occurred to me, there was some pretty mean characters in this world. It made me glad that not many of them ever found their way to Whiskey City.

About a quarter of the way through the stack, I found one on Butch. Reading through it, I let out a whistle. One thing you had to say for ol' Butch, he wasn't lazy. If he'd done half the things he was wanted for, he'd kept right busy. According to the flyer, he'd robbed a couple of banks, stuck up some stages, and generally made a nuisance of himself.

A couple of flyers down the stack, I came across one on Hetfield. Reading the Wanted poster on Hetfield, I realized that next to Hetfield, Butch was a Sunday school teacher. About the nicest thing Hetfield ever done was shoot a man in the foot.

Pushing the rest of the stack away, I studied the flyers on Butch and Hetfield. I figured if I wanted to go through the whole stack, I could find posters on Red and Skinny, but they were small potatoes.

Hetfield fascinated me. Every time I thought of

those cool, gray eyes and that thin, cruel face, I felt a shiver. Knowing Hetfield was in the neighborhood was like walking in tall weeds and knowing a rattler was underfoot.

Hetfield was wanted in Kansas for murdering an entire family for a little stash of money they kept hidden under their floorboards. As far as I could tell, he wasn't wanted here in Wyoming, but that was probably because he'd never been here before.

I read both flyers several times, trying to learn how the pair thought and catch a glint of their methods. The only thing I learned was that they were dangerous, desperate men. Killing didn't bother them, for about every job they pulled they killed someone.

After wadding up both flyers, I stuffed them in my pocket. I sat at my desk staring out the window for a long time, not sure I was equipped to tackle a pair like Butch and Hetfield.

Leaving the stack of Wanted posters lying on the desk, I walked outside. Remembering Wiesmulluer's idea to find Butch's camp, I hurried down to the stable to fetch my horse. I found him in his stall, quietly eating feed from the bunk. Pulling him out of the stall, I slapped my saddle on and mounted up.

Riding out of the stable, I pulled up and looked around. If I wanted to watch the town from a spot of concealment, where would be the best spot? Turning my head slowly, I let my eyes wander over the country surrounding Whiskey City. To effectively watch the town, they would choose high ground. Most of the country around the town was open, offering little in the way of cover.

The knoll behind the stable presented the most likely option. Turley's old dugout was built into the face of the knoll, and a draw ran just behind it. A group of men and their horses could hide in the draw while one man kept watch on the town from the top.

Lifting the reins, I urged my horse forward. I felt a wave of sadness as I rode past Turley's dugout. In all the excitement, I hadn't realized how much I was going to miss the old trapper. Turley had a way of livening things up when ever he was in town.

"I guess you're still livening things up," I said as I rode up the hill past the dugout. "It's your darn gold mine that started this whole mess."

At the top of the knoll, I slid off my horse and started crisscrossing the area, casting about for a sign. I patrolled the area for an hour, my eyes glued to the ground. Finally, I found a spot on top of the knoll where someone had indeed watched the town, but even though the tracks looked vaguely familiar, they didn't belong to Butch or any of his gang. I'd take an oath on that.

Down in the draw, I found a spot where the man had camped. He'd spent several days in the camp, watching the town. Even so, he'd left mighty little sign. Whoever the man was, he could hide a trail. Going over the ground again, I decided that not only could this man hide a trail, but doing so was second nature to him.

Taking off my hat, I wiped the sweat from my face. A man who hid his trail out of habit sounded like an outlaw to me. Climbing back to the top of the knoll, I looked down upon Whiskey City, mentally reviewing what I'd learned about the man. He had a long, easy stride, too long to be the stocky Red. His tracks didn't cut deep enough to be those of either Hetfield or Butch, who were both good-sized men. Skinny? No. This this man was quick and light on his feet. Skinny was a plodder. When I trailed them away from the bank, I noticed Skinny's tracks were always smudged, like he drug his feet.

No, this was someone else. Whoever this man was, I didn't think his presence meant good things to come for me or Whiskey City.

Mounting my horse, I rode back down to town as the sun sank low in the west. I wished I could have found the camp of Butch and his men. Butch and Hetfield, they didn't strike me as the type of men to give up on a notion. They would be back, and they wouldn't be in a visiting mood. They'd be back to take another whack at the bank, I'd bet my whole wad on that. And when they came back, I had better be ready, or I'd likely end getting my mail in Boot Hill.

Whiskey City looked like a ghost town as I rode down the street. A restless wind stirred the dust in front of me, but that was the only movement on the street. Every soul in town must have been out looking for that map.

Stabling my horse, I gave him a quick rubdown, then hurried back to the hotel. While I washed up, I thought about going to Wiesmulluer's in the morning. When I left, the town would be deserted. Everybody was out looking for that map. Shoot, Butch could ride up and load the whole bank on a wagon, one piece at a time if he wanted. There wouldn't be anyone in town to stop him. And I wasn't forgetting about Bobby Stamper. I still wasn't sure I trusted him.

Drying off, I slipped on a fresh shirt, then hurried down to the lobby, afraid that Lilly would be waiting on me, but the lobby was as empty as

Mother Hubbard's cupboard, so I took a seat and waited.

I waited, squirming in my chair for twenty minutes before Lilly appeared at the top of the stairs. Looking up at her, I had to catch my breath.

She stood poised and graceful, like a queen surveying her court. Carrying her head high and with one hand gliding on the banister, she floated down the stairs.

She stopped at the bottom of the stairs, waiting while I clambered to my feet. Arm in arm, we walked into the dining room. On the outside, I was trying to look all unconcerned, like this was something I did every day, but on the inside I was wound tighter than a dimestore clock.

We'd barely sat down at a table before Blanche slapped a couple of cups of coffee down in front of us. Lilly glanced at her cup, then up at Blanche. "Do you have tea? If you do, I would prefer it."

"Coffee's what we got," Blanche said, looking sour as raw lemons. "If you want to eat, we got beef and cornbread."

"That will be fine," Lilly said, smiling as Blanche walked away grumbling. "She's full of good cheer this evening."

"She didn't used to be thataway. She used to be the nicest, sweetest person you could ever meet," I said, shaking my head. "I swear, since word got out about that mine, the whole town's went plumb loco."

"The mine is what I wanted to speak to you about," Lilly said, covering my hand with both of hers. "You see, I feel that the mine rightfully belongs to me. It belonged to my husband, and whatever was his was also mine."

Lilly stroked my hand, looking into my face with

a pair of bewitching green eyes. "Turley, bless his heart, he thought he left me well taken care of, and, in fact, he did leave me a lot of money, but he also left a lot of debts."

Lilly laughed, but she sounded more sad than happy. "If you knew Turley, then you know how he was with money; if he didn't have any on him, he borrowed. He knew people all over the country, and he must have borrowed from all of them. By the time I squared all his debts, I was broke."

Lilly's face turned sad, and a tear formed in the corner of her eye. She dabbed at her eye with a lacy handkerchief. "I'm sorry. I always get this way when I think of Turley being gone. I am just now beginning to realize how much I miss him."

Blanche plopped our plates down in front of us, snorting rather indelicately. I shot her a mean look, thinking she could show more compassion to someone obviously struck with grief. Blanche didn't pay me no mind; she simply tossed our knives and forks on the table. "If you want more coffee, the pot's on the stove," she informed us and marched away.

Lilly swabbed her eyes again, giving me a brave little smile. "I'm sorry, Sheriff. It's just so overwhelming at times," she said, patting my hand. "What I'm asking is, that if the mine is found, you see that it is turned over to me. After all, I am the rightful owner. Of course, I'd be willing to pay the person who finds the mine a handsome fee."

I couldn't say no. I looked into that lovely face, so sad, and I wanted to do all I could for her. I felt like rushing right out and finding that mine that very minute. "Don't you fret, ma'am, I'll see that you get what's coming to you," I promised, straightening up in my chair. "I'm the law in these parts, and folks around here listen to me. I'll convince them to hand over your fair share."

"I'm sure you will. It was fortunate for me to find a man as strong and brave as you," Lilly said, smiling sweetly. "And handsome too. You are a very attractive man, Sheriff."

I reckon I was beaming from ear to ear. I squared my shoulders and puffed out my chest, wishing I was ten men so I could do more for her. "Don't you worry about a thing, ma'am. I'll take of everything."

"You're very kind, but please call me Lilly."

We finished our supper, and Lilly didn't eat much. She just poked and pushed at her food. Me, on the other hand, I ate everything that I could saw up and stuff down my throat.

As I slicked up my plate, Lilly pushed hers away. "This has been a long day. I think I'll retire to my room," she said quietly.

Pushing back my chair, I walked Lilly up to her room. We stopped at her door, Lilly turning to face me. "Thank you for the dinner, Sheriff," she said, looking weepy again.

"Aw, I was happy to do it," I said, twisting my hat in my hands. "And don't worry; I'll do my best to help you."

All at once, Lilly came up against me, circling her arms around my waist and leaning her head against my chest. "I know you will," she said softly. "It's just that I feel so alone. If I don't get that mine . . . I don't know what I'll do," she added in a choked voice. I could feel her body shudder as she sobbed against my chest.

Feeling as awkward as a polar bear in a tea room, I reached around her and patted her on the back. "It'll be okay, I'll make sure of it."

Lilly raised her head to look up at my face. Her eyes were red and tears streamed down her cheeks. "I know you will do what you can. I'm counting on you."

Wiping the tears from her face, she gave me a brave smile. "Good night, Sheriff," she said, and rushed into her he room.

Right then, I started to get sore. It wasn't right for a woman like Miss Lilly to have such troubles. I made up my mind to see that she got that mine.

Despite my resolve, a doubt snuck into my mind as I walked away from her door. The folks of this town had their hearts set on that mine, and talking them out of it wouldn't be easy. What I'd told Lilly wasn't true, the people of this town never listened to me. To them, I was a big, overgrown kid who didn't know nothing from nothing.

Andrews now, he never shared a dollar in his life. What if he was the one that found the map? Or Iris and Gid? Iris was hard as nails and twice as mean. More than that, she was stingy as a hungry wolf. I began to wonder if I'd made a promise I couldn't keep.

I decided to wander down to the saloon. I figured the treasure hunters would be gathered there. Maybe I could convince them to give half the mine to Lilly, once it was found. Sure, that was the ticket. If there was as much gold in that mine as everyone thought, nobody should mind giving up half, and half should be plenty to fix Miss Lilly up.

Hoping I'd found the answer, I hurried out of the hotel. It was a beautiful night. A full moon hung in the sky, lighting the street with a soft glow.

Liking the feel of the night, I stood on the board-walk soaking it up. That's when I heard the noise. It was a thumping sound, like somebody dropped something heavy.

Cocking my ears, I eased down the street toward the noise. I was in front of the bank when I heard it again, followed by a *shushing* sound.

Someone was inside the bank!

A bolt of fear shot through me, freezing me dead in my tracks. A lump sprang to my throat, and a cold ball of fear settled heavily in my belly.

Lifting one foot slowly, I took a cautious step. The bank was silent as a grave now. Trying not to make a sound, I catfooted it over to the corner of the building. Pressing my body to the wall, I stretched my neck out, straining to see in the window.

Through the gloom, I saw a shadowy figure move inside. Snapping my head back, I sucked up against the wall. My heart going all out, I tried to work up the courage to do what I had to do. I glanced down at my hands, which trembled slightly.

Deep inside me, I knew who was in there— Butch and his bunch of cutthroats! The thought of facing them chilled my blood. Especially Hetfield. To tell the truth, the pale-faced Hetfield scared the life out of me.

I wanted to run, my mind screamed for me to run, but I couldn't do it. This was what the town paid me for. Besides, what would folks think of me if I ran from trouble? Breathing a silent prayer, and holding my back against the building, I edged around back. When I came to the side door, I stepped away from the wall. Screwing my eyes shut, I clenched my fists, trying to steady myself.

I blew out a big sigh and raised my booted foot. Kicking open the door, I lunged inside, my eyes peering through the darkness. I saw the shadowy figure of a man dart across the bank and duck behind an overturned desk. My breath caught in my throat, as my hand swooped down to my pistol. Fighting the fear that threatened to claim me, I clawed at the butt of my pistol. The pistol seemed to be stuck, so I rared back and gave a big jerk.

I'd forgotten to loosen the thong again, and when I jerked I broke the thong. The pistol flew from my grip, spinning across the room. I heard a loud grunt as the gun flew behind the desk.

All of a sudden, I realized I was standing smack-dab in the middle of the room with no gun. Fear welling up inside me, I dove for cover.

"Sheriff, look out!" a squawky voice called out. That's when I noticed that the safe I'd taken cover behind was about to explode.

Chapter Seven

It was too dark for me to see the dynamite, but I sure saw the fuse burning toward the safe. Even dumb as I am sometimes, I recognized the fuse for what it was and knew that I didn't want to be hug-gin' that safe when it went *Boom!* Pushing away from the safe, I scrambled across the floor. I managed a couple of bounds before she went pop.

The sound of that explosion dang near split my head wide open, and the blast sorta picked me up and flung me right out the front window. I lit smack-dab in the middle of the street.

Rolling over, I saw the dangdest sight I ever did see, or ever hope to. That safe had been blown right through the roof. It was a good ten feet above the building and still going up, leaving a trail of sparks behind. That iron box shot up almost twenty feet above the bank, then it stopped. It hung there for a second, then turned over and fell. It crashed to the ground with the speed of a bullet. While I couldn't see where it hit, the sight of boards flying up in the air led me to believe it landed on the outhouse in the alley.

My ears ringing like church bells on Easter Sunday, I staggered to my feet, coughing up smoke. For a minute I swayed, fighting for balance on wobbly legs.

A crowd of folks poured out of the saloon, waving and pointing. I saw their lips flapping and their jaws working overtime, but I'll be danged if I could hear a word they said.

Stamper rushed over, shouting in my ear. "What the devil happened?"

His voice floated into my ear like it was from a dream, and I could barely hear it. "Somebody tried to rob the bank!" I shouted back, digging in my ear with my finger.

Right away, folks went to pulling guns, and commenced to blasting away. "Come out with your hands up!" Andrews shouted when they stopped to reload.

My hearing musta been returning, 'cause I heard someone inside call out. "For God's sake, don't shoot. We're coming out."

As one, the crowd took a step back, leveling their guns at the door, or what was left of it. I must say, that door had taken a beating the last few days. After I crashed through it, Andrews had nailed it back in place, nailing some boards across it to keep it there. Now, it hung cockeyed, fastened only in one corner.

A booted foot appeared, cautiously kicking the ruined door out of the way, then two people stepped from the bank. For a second, we didn't recognize them, but when we did, a gasp traveled through the crowd, followed by a lot of whispering.

Standing on the boardwalk in front of the bank,

smoke rising from their hair and clothes and their faces singed and blackened by smoke, were Iris and Gid. Gid had my pistol and a knot on his head. Holding the barrel with two fingers, he solemnly extended the weapon to me.

"Iris! Gid!" Andrews sputtered, sounding shocked. "What's the meaning of this?"

"We thought the map might be in the safe, so we decided to have a look," Gid said, hanging his head.

A charge whipped through the throng of people standing in the street. "Well, was it?" Claude asked, his voice strained.

"Aw, crud, we don't know," Iris said disgustedly. "I told you this wouldn't work, you nincompoop," she added, whacking Gid across the head and shoulders.

"What happened to my safe?" Andrews asked, his voice almost pleading.

Iris quit beating on Gid, her face turning wooden as she simply pointed straight up with a bony finger.

"You should have seen it," I said. "That safe went through the roof like a greased pig. It hit in the alley. I'd say it wiped out the outhouse."

"What!" Joe Havens yelled. "Burdett was in there!" he screamed, sprinting for the alley.

Like a stampeding herd, the rest of us pounded along behind him. We swept around the corner amid a fog of dust. A hush settled over us when we saw the outhouse smashed flat as a cowchip in the middle of the road.

Perched majestically on top of that pile of splintered lumber rested Andrews's fancy safe. It didn't look so fancy now, not scorched and scarred like it was. Just looking at the outhouse, we could tell there wasn't any way in the world anyone inside could have survived.

Slowly we drug off our hats, bowing our heads. "Burdett was a cantankerous cuss, but he was a good smith," Joe Havens said, sniffling.

"He'll be sorely missed," Claude agreed sadly.

"Boy! Talk about your bad breaks," Stamper said, shaking his head. "What a way to go."

As we gave Burdett his eulogy, a board came flying up out of the wreckage. Right before our unbelieving eyes, Burdett began to emerge from the rubble. He came out slowly, batting boards outta the way. Nobody moved to help him. I guess we were too surprised to see him still alive.

Finally, the shock wore off, and we rushed forward, jerking him out of the wreck. Burdett's eyes were glassed over and his whole face sagged. "What happened?" he mumbled, and would have fallen if I hadn't caught him.

"It was Iris and Gid!" Joe Havens declared hotly, pointing an accusing finger at the pair. "They up and decided to rob the bank, and danged near got you kilt in the process."

"Hogwash, he looks fine to me," Iris said, waving her hands at Joe.

"Fine!" Joe screamed, gesturing wildly at Burdett. "Look at him. He looks like he seen a ghost or became one, which he durn near did."

"Bah, he's always looked goofy to me." Iris sneered.

"Anyway, we weren't trying to rob the bank. We just wanted to look inside the safe to see if the map might be there," Gid explained meekly.

"It was Gid's fool idea to shove a bushel basket of dynamite under the safe and light the fuse," Iris said, branding Gid with a searing look.

Andrews had been hugging the safe like that hunk of iron was his firstborn. Now he looked up angrily. He barreled down off that stack of wood, shoving Gid in the chest. "Didn't you stop to think that if the map had been in the safe, I would have known about it?" he asked, his tone wailing.

"We thought maybe Turley left some of his important papers with you for safekeeping and that the map was among them," Gid explained.

"Turley never left any papers with me, and if he had, I would have already went through them," Andrews replied.

Iris sniffed, poking her nose in the air. She glared at Andrews, then spun on her heels, walking away without looking back. Gid shuffled his feet, his head bobbing about nervously. Ramming his hands in his pockets, he ducked his head, following Iris like a lost puppy.

"Aren't you going to arrest them, Sheriff?" Bobby Stamper asked innocently.

"I don't know," I replied slowly. To tell the truth, I hadn't thought about that. Arrest Iris Winkler and Gid Stevens! Talk about a shocker.

"You sure would have arrested me, if I had done this," Stamper pointed out sarcastically, but judging from the smile on his face, he enjoyed stirring up trouble.

Still, Stamper had a point. If he had done this, I'd already have him locked up. Why, I chased Butch and his men all day, and they didn't do half the damage that Iris and Gid managed to accomplish.

"What do you guys think?" I asked, looking at the group.

Mr. Claude shrugged, giving me a sympathetic

pat on the shoulder. "I understand your problem. Iris and Gid are good people, and they weren't actually trying to rob anyone. They were just looking for the map. Still, they did try to blow up the bank."

"Try, my butt. I'd say they got the job done," Joe declared.

He was right too. A week ago, the bank was probably the nicest building in town, but it was a sorry-looking affair now. Both doors were gone, leaving jagged holes in the walls. Every window in the place was shattered, and a gaping hole had been torn in the roof. Most likely the roof would cave in the first high wind.

"Aren't you going after them?" Andrews asked.

"I don't think so," I answered, looking down the alley in the direction the pair took.

All of a sudden, Andrews lost interest in coddling that safe. "What?" he yelled, jumping up and waving his arms like he was trying to raise up a windstorm. "They tried to steal my money!"

"Aw, shoot, this is Iris and Gid we're talking about. They ain't going anywhere. When I decide what needs to be done about this mess, I'll know where to find them," I said, impatience putting an edge on my voice.

"That's for sure. You can bet they ain't leaving town. Least not until that map is found," Claude agreed.

"Well, I'm glad we cleared that up. I'd say it was high time for a drink," Stamper suggested, grinning from ear to ear. "Besides, I think this man needs a bracer," he added, pointing to Burdett, who was staggering around in circles.

"Let's get him into the saloon," Joe said, steering Burdett in the right direction.

"What about my safe?" Andrews protested as we trooped toward the saloon. "We need to move it back inside."

Stamper cast a critical eye from where the safe rested to what was left of the bank building. "It don't look like moving it back into the bank would be much of an improvement," he observed dryly.

"How about carting it into the saloon. I don't feel right leaving it out in the alley," Andrews suggested hopefully.

Andrews's suggestion fell on deaf ears, and we kept walking. "I'll stand for a round of drinks," he offered.

That grabbed everyone's attention. Joe propped Burdett against the wall of the bank while we gathered around the safe. "How in the devil are we going to move this thing? It weighs more than a team of horses," Stamper wondered, trying to lift one corner of the safe.

"Get some ropes and string them underneath the safe," Claude suggested.

Nobody had a better idea, so we hunted up a couple of lariats and worked them under the safe. Mr. Claude and I took the ends of the front rope while Joe and Stamper manned the back one.

Andrews stood back, like a king, waiting till we were ready. "Okay, on three, everyone heave," he instructed. "One, two, three, heave!" he shouted.

We bowed our backs and lifted. It took some doing, but we hoisted the safe off the ground. Staggering under the weight, we drug the box into the saloon.

We stood it up in the back corner, then crossed to the bar. Joe was pouring our drinks when a glazed-over and groggy Burdett stumbled into the saloon. "What happened?" he asked, clutching the bar for support.

"Never mind. Drink this," Joe instructed, sliding him a drink. "You boys ready for a belt?"

We were, except for Stamper, who still stood in front of the safe, staring at it with a gleam in his eyes.

Taking my drink and his, I crossed to the safe. "Could you really open that thing?" I asked, handing him his drink.

Stamper shrugged, taking the drink. "Who knows," he said, taking a sip. He shot me a smile. "Maybe I'll try sometime."

I knew Stamper was trying to get under my skin, so I ignored him and returned to the bar. "You boys hear Turley's widow is in town?" I asked.

"No, what's she like?" Joe asked.

"Very nice-looking. In fact, I'd say she was down right beautiful," I told them, and I could tell they didn't believe it. I stared down in my glass, swirling the whiskey as I picked my words carefully. "She claims that no matter what Turley's will said, the mine belongs to her, and she wants it," I said, looking up to catch their reaction.

Stunned looks crossed their faces, but anger quickly replaced the surprise. "No way," Joe Havens stated flatly. "That mine was Turley's to do with as he pleased, and he left it to whoever finds it!"

"That's right!" Andrews agreed, slapping the bar with his hand.

"I don't know, but Miss Lilly claims that since the mine belonged to her husband it also belonged to her, and she wants it."

"Turley found that mine. He could do with it as he saw fit," Mr. Claude said.

"Turley left it to whoever finds it, and I think the only decent thing to do is honor his wishes," Andrews said gravely.

"Lilly—is that Turley's wife's name?" Stamper asked, rubbing his chin. "What's her last name?"

I looked at him, like he was off his rocker. "Simmons, of course," I told him.

Stamper grinned ruefully back at me. "Yeah, I guess it would be. What did she look like?"

"Like I said, she was a looker. Lots of yeller hair piled high on her head and green eyes."

Stamper nodded, holding his hand out about shoulder height. "Pale skin, about this tall?"

"That's her. Do you know her?"

A crafty look sprang to Stamper's eyes as he grinned and waved his hand. "Naw, I just seen her around town and was curious."

I didn't believe him, not for an instant, but I didn't press it. I'd learned enough to know that when Bobby Stamper decided to keep something under his hat, that's what he did.

"What are you going to do about this woman's claim?" Claude wanted to know.

I shook my head, finishing my drink. "I ain't exactly figured that out yet. Maybe I'll have a chat with that lawyer, Thomas. He could tell me what's the legal thing to do," I said, and decided to do just that.

Pushing my empty glass away, I left the saloon. Yawning, I strolled to the hotel. The lobby was empty, so I helped myself, opening the register. I found Thomas's name, and the book said he was staying in room 6.

As I climbed the stairs, I wondered if I should wait until morning. It was already past midnight. I stopped in the hall, thinking it over. It was late, but

if I was going out to Wiesmulluer's in the morning
I'd have to leave before sunup and wouldn't get
back until evening. Deciding I didn't want to wait
that long, I stepped up to Thomas's door and hammered on it.

Looking idly down the hall, I waited impatiently.
When Thomas didn't answer, I banged on the door
again. I waited a moment, then tried the knob.

The door wasn't locked, and swung open under
my touch. Lighting a match, I stepped inside, calling softly to the lawyer. Crossing to the nightstand,
I lit the lamp. As light flooded the room, I looked
around.

The bed was still made, and a fancy suit lay
across the end of the bed. Thomas's valise sat in
the corner, and a stack of papers rested on the
nightstand. It looked like he had just stepped out
for a moment. And that didn't make no sense.

Sitting on the corner of the bed, I tried to figure
out where he could be. I just came from the saloon
and he wasn't there, and in Whiskey City at this
hour there just wasn't any other place he could be.

Chapter Eight

The next morning, I was up and around well before the sun. Hunching my shoulders against the chill and wishing I had brought a jacket, I pointed my horse toward the Wiesmulluer ranch, riding slowly out of town. As the sun crept over the horizon, I fought to shed the sleepiness that dogged me. I swear, me and my bed were becoming strangers. Just offhand, I couldn't remember the last time I slept eight good hours.

Not last night, that's for sure. After I left Thomas's room, I made the rounds of town, but the lawyer was nowhere to be found. This morning, I checked his room again, finding it exactly as I left it the night before.

Thinking it over, I decided there was something about that whole deal didn't set right. If he went somewhere, why didn't he take his stuff? It crossed my mind that maybe he had been kidnapped. Perhaps somebody took the notion that Thomas knew where the map was and hauled the lawyer out of town to beat the location out of him.

Thomas's room looked neat, not like there had been any trouble. 'Course, Thomas was a scrawny feller. Maybe he didn't have it in him to put up much of a scrap.

All this thinking was doing nothing but giving me a headache, so I quit worrying about it and concentrated on enjoying the ride. I rode into the Wiesmulluer yard about midmorning.

Marie Wiesmulluer was hanging clothes on the line, glancing up as I rode in. Betsy stood on the porch, looking pretty enough to take my breath away. "Good morning, Teddy," she said, her voice sounding like the wind sifting through the canyons.

I just sat on my horse, staring down at her. "Your pa said I should come out," I finally managed to stammer.

Betsy gave me a dazzling smile. "Did you do any thinking about what I said?"

"You mean about being rich?" I asked. "You were talking about Turley's mine?"

"Of course I was, silly," she replied, leaning across the porch railing. "Bobby told me all about it at the dance the other night. I think he wanted to impress me. If he finds the map, you could take it from him. Then we could go back east together and live in style."

Betsy looked up at me, her eyes wide, and her smile making me woozy. Her words came to me like a dream, giving me a glimpse of heaven.

"Sheriff," Mrs. Wiesmulluer said, carrying her basket of clothes. She gave me a disapproving look, but her voice was friendly. "Karl has already left, but Eddy will show you where the steer was killed. She's down at the barn.''

"Thank you," I said, turning my horse down to the barn. Leaving the reins trailing in the dust, I dismounted outside the barn. Walking inside, I saw Eddy brushing the coat of a red colt. Judging from the shine of that coat, I'd say she'd been at it a while.

Leaning on a stable partition, I watched her work, admiring her gracefulness and the gentle way she handled the spirited colt.

She must have sensed my presence because she whirled around. "How long have you been there gawking at me?" she demanded.

"Not long. You do that like you know how," I remarked, hoping a compliment might soften her mood.

It didn't. She dropped her brush and comb into a bucket, wiping her hands on her shirt. "Did you come out here to flap your jaws or do your job?" she asked, stepping out of the stall. "I realize we are just ordinary folks, hardly worthy of your time. We don't have fancy clothes and hairdos. Why, it's a wonder you even have time for us at all."

"You should be more considerate. Miss Lilly is a grieving widow," I said sternly.

"Ha! Conniving widow is more like it," Eddy shot right back. "Well, let's go. I'll show you the place."

I waited while she fetched her horse. Then we rode out of the yard side by side, neither of us saying a word. "What did you mean? I mean, the part about Lilly being a conniving widow? She seems real nice to me."

Eddy gave me a long hard look. "Teddy, I

swear, you're dumber than a post sometimes,'' she said, sounding exasperated.

Well, maybe I was, but that still didn't answer my question. I opened my mouth to ask her again, then slammed it back shut. If she was going to be so persnickety about it, then I didn't want her opinion.

No sir, I didn't give two hoots about what she thought. We rode aways, and I kept glancing over at Eddy, expecting her to break down and say what she had to say. Before long, I broke down. I just couldn't take the strain. I had to know, and before long my curiosity got the better of me and I asked again.

Eddy stopped her horse, patting his neck as she stared across the saddle at me. "I'll bet you the reason Lilly is here is she wants that mine."

"She said she was broke," I replied, feeling the need to defend Miss Lilly.

Eddy laughed, still petting her horse. "Sure thing, any fool can see poor Miss Lilly doesn't have a dollar to her name. Imagine having to walk down the street in them rags she was wearing."

I didn't say anything as we started our horses back in motion. "All right, maybe you are right. Maybe Miss Lilly isn't dead broke," I conceded. "But she claims the mine is hers since it belonged to her husband."

"Ha! You don't you even know Turley was her husband."

"She told me so," I replied. "Besides, Turley mentioned a wife in his will."

"That doesn't mean she was the one." Eddy tossed her hair, laughing. "Tell me, did she have a ring?"

For the life of me, I couldn't recall seeing one.

Dang woman, why'd she have to be right all the time? Sighing, I gave up. "Okay, I guess I need to talk to that lawyer, Thomas. He'd know if Lilly and Turley was married."

"Why don't you do that?" Eddy asked.

"I'd like to, but I can't find him," I grumbled.

Eddy pulled up, stretching her arm out to point. "There it is," she said, and I could make out the remains of the steer.

"Stay back until I get a chance to look around," I instructed, handing her my reins. She made a face at me, but took the reins and sat quietly.

I circled the dead steer, my eyes glued to the ground. I walked two complete circles around the animal before approaching it. Rubbing my chin, I squatted beside the dead steer. I'd found tracks, but they weren't what I expected. I'd been expecting the tracks of the square-toed boots that Claude always wore, but these were different. Fact was, these were the same tracks as the man who'd been watching Whiskey City.

I looked hard, but I couldn't find any sign of where he'd approached the animal. The ones leading away, however, were plain as day. Whoever the man was, he'd shot the animal, butchered it, loaded the meat, then rode away, his trail leading plainly for Claude's farm.

Taking off my hat, I sat down on a rock. "This wasn't Mr. Claude who done this," I said, looking up at Eddy.

Eddy smiled sweetly down at me. "Of course not. We wouldn't have called you out had it been Mr. Claude," she said, and while her smile looked sweet her tone sure wasn't. Eddy tossed down her reins and mine as she dropped lightly off her horse.

"Are you going to follow the trail?" she asked, taking a seat beside me.

"I don't reckon."

Eddy frowned. "You'd better. Pa's expecting you to find the man that did this," she warned.

"I don't have to follow the trail. I got a good idea where to find this man," I said, and couldn't help sounding smug about it.

For once, it was Eddy's turn to look confused. "Did you recognize the tracks? Pa looked at them, and they didn't mean anything to him."

"I never said I knew who killed your steer, but I might know where his hideout is," I corrected. "You remember when your pa told me that I should find the camp where Butch and his men stayed?"

"So it was one of them," Eddy said, jumping in before I could finish my thought.

"No," I said, giving her a smug smile. Now I'd show her that she wasn't as smart as she thought. "While I was looking for their camp, I found some tracks on the ridge behind the stable. You know, the one where that old dugout is? Anyway, I found the tracks of one man. He's been up on the ridge watching the town."

"What do you mean watching the town?"

"He had a camp in the draw just behind the ridge, but he spent most of his time up on the ridge. I found the spot where he waited, in a little nest of rocks."

"Why in the world would anyone want to set up on that ridge and do nothing but watch the town?" Eddy wondered.

I shrugged my shoulders, looking to the mountains in the distance. "If I were guessing, I'd say it had something to do with Turley's map."

"If you don't know who it was, how can you be sure it is the same man that killed our steer?"

"Come here. I'll show you," I said, taking her hand. I led her over to the dead animal. "You see where he squatted. Notice the cut in the sole of his left boot?"

"Right there on the edge, up next to the toe?" Eddy asked.

"Yeah, now look at the tracks of his horse. Three of the shoes have a cleat and the fourth is smooth. Well, that's the same as the man on the ridge."

Eddy frowned, looking down at the tracks of the horse. "Whoever he is, he must live around here," she decided.

"How do you figure that?" I asked, wondering what I missed.

"He knew enough about the area to make it look like Mr. Claude done this. He must have known that Pa lets Mr. Claude butcher a beef every now and again."

"That makes sense, I guess. All I know is that I wish they would hurry up and find that map so things can get back to normal."

"What about you? Have you been looking for the map?"

"Not really. I guess I've done some thinking about what I'd do if I found it, but I've 'bout decided I don't want the thing." I pulled up a tuft of grass, rolling it between my fingers. "It seems to me that whoever finds the map and the mine is stuck with it. They'll spend all their time either digging the gold or guarding the mine. I don't want that."

"What do you want?" Eddy asked, her voice barely a whisper.

"I'd like to get my father's place back. Raise some cattle, maybe a few crops."

"How about a family? Don't you want a family?"

"Sure I do," I answered, looking over at her. I wanted to tell her that she was the one I wanted to raise that family with. Clearing my throat, I tried to work up the courage to tell her. I opened my mouth and the words almost came out, but then my nerve deserted me. My shoulders sagging, I tossed away the bit of grass. "Aw, what does is matter? I'm not likely to ever get the money to buy the place back," I said miserably.

Plumb disgusted with myself, I stood up. "We better be getting back," I said gruffly.

We rode in silence a long time, me kicking myself for not having the gumption to say what was on my mind. Several times, I stole a glance across at Eddy, but she seemed lost in her own thoughts.

"You wouldn't necessarily have to buy your father's place back. The West is full of land, just there for the taking," she said suddenly. "The place wouldn't matter, not as long as you were with the ones you loved."

"That's true," I said slowly, feeling my throat tighten up. "I always did want a place up in the mountains."

"One of those little valleys with running water," Eddy agreed, closing her eyes.

"Yeah, a big house surrounded by trees, and a garden in the back," I said, thinking she would fit nicely into the picture. I glanced at her, trying to screw up my nerve to say what I was thinking, but we reached the house before I got it done.

Old man Wiesmulluer almost came uncorked when we rode into the yard. He was tying his horse in front of the house when he spotted us. Dropping the reins, he charged away from the house, cussing and flapping his arms so hard I thought he'd take off flying.

"What are you doing here?" he roared. "You're supposed to be out tracking down the varmint who's been killing my cows."

All of his screeching and flapping around was spooking my horse, and I had to clamp down on the reins to keep the animal from bolting. "Take it easy, Mr. Wiesmulluer," I said, trying to calm both him and my horse at the same time.

"Take it easy, my foot," Wiesmulluer fumed, wiping his mouth on his sleeve. "I can't afford to lose any more cattle!"

"The reason I ain't chasing the man is because I know where I can find him," I explained patiently. Okay, I'll admit that maybe I was stretching the truth a mite, but I wanted to calm him down.

Some of the fire left his eyes as he cocked his head, gazing at me with an appraising eye. "You know who done it?" he asked, sounding like he couldn't believe that I did.

"Maybe," I said, and explained to him about the tracks I found.

As I talked, the old coot calmed down a bit. He actually seemed pleased that I'd followed his advice. "Any idea who the polecat is?" he asked gruffly.

"No, but I reckon he's got something to do with the map."

Wiesmulluer snorted, kicking the ground. "Turley's gold mine? If you ask me, this whole mess is just another one of Turley's fool pranks."

"His wife seems to think the mine is real enough," I countered.

"I never knew he had a wife," Wiesmulluer said grumpily.

"Yeah, I seen her. She seems nice," I said and drew a murderous look from Eddy. I was beginning to realize that around Eddy I best not mention Lilly.

Wiesmulluer rubbed his chin, frowning darkly. "Makes no never mind," he decided. "I still say this is more of Turley's foolishness. He never did have a lick of sense. You recall the time he put blasting powder in Burdett's forge?"

Boy, did I! It took a month for Burdett's eyebrows to grow back. Shaking my head, I had to laugh. Turley had always been up to something.

"I don't know if there is a mine or not, but everyone in town believes it. I swear, they've all gone plumb crazy. Last night, Iris and Gid blew up the bank."

"What?" Eddy and her pa yelled at the same time.

"They thought the map might be in the safe, so they up and decided to take a peek," I explained.

"Did they find the map?" Eddy asked, breathlessly.

I glanced sharply at her, hoping that she wasn't catching the craziness that was going around. "They didn't know what they were doing. Instead of blowing the safe open, they shot it right through the roof."

A low chuckle escaped past Wiesmulluer's lips. I had to bat myself in the head and dig a finger in my ear just to make sure I really heard it. Why, I couldn't hardly remember ever seeing the old goat smile, much less laugh out loud.

"I'd give a peck of powder muffins to see that,"

Wiesmulluer said, chuckling again. "I bet ol' Andrews about had a conniption."

"He wasn't happy," I admitted, eyeing him warily. I didn't trust his sudden good mood. "He really raised a row; allowed that I should toss them in jail."

"You didn't, did you?" Eddy asked, her hand going to her mouth. "I couldn't imagine poor Iris in jail."

"Do the old bat some good," Wiesmulluer grumbled.

"Papa! What a thing to say," Eddy scolded. "Teddy, don't you listen to him. You can't put that poor woman in jail."

"I wasn't figuring on it," I admitted, but deep down, I shared Wiesmulluer's opinion. A day or two in the can would put a dent in her sharp tongue. "The way I see it, if Gid and Iris will pay to fix the bank, that should be all there is to it."

As Wiesmulluer nodded his agreement, Betsy came to the door, calling them to dinner. Betsy smiled, giving me a little wave. I noticed the quick flash of anger that streaked across Eddy's face as I returned the wave.

"You want to join us?" Wiesmulluer invited, waving a hand in the direction of the house.

I durn near fell down, I was so shocked. I batted my eyes a couple of times, just to make sure it was the old man Wiesmulluer that made the offer. "I sure would like to, but I best be getting back to town," I said slowly. "With all that's happened, I don't like being away."

Wiesmulluer nodded, scrunching up his eyebrows and rubbing his hands on his shirt. "Eddy, run on inside. I want to talk with the sheriff alone," Wiesmulluer ordered.

Eddy started to argue, but a scowl from the old man set her feet in motion. "See you later, Teddy," she said, giving me a wave.

Wiesmulluer rubbed his chin, taking my elbow and leading me away from the house. "I got something to tell you and I didn't want to say anything in front of Eddy," he said as I twisted around, waving to Eddy on the porch. "Those four men you was trailing, they's back. I ran across their trail yesterday."

He had my attention now. "You mean the ones that tried to rob the bank?" I asked.

Wiesmulluer nodded, stopping and turning to face me. "Fact is, I saw them and what's more, I recognized one of them. The blonde one, I saw him before."

"Hetfield!" I whispered, my voice hoarse and a shiver racing up my spine.

"That's him," Wiesmulluer agreed, nodding grimly. "I don't know if you remember, but it was eight years ago when we were outfitting our wagons to come west. I saw that Hetfield in Kansas. They was fixing to hang him, and from what I heard, he deserved it too.

"No, sir, I don't remember. My folks weren't part of that wagon train."

A frown crossed Wiesmulluer's lips and his whole face pinched up. "Yeah, I forgot that your folks didn't come out here till a year or so later." Wiesmulluer shook his head. "Anyway, like I said, they was fixin' to hang this Hetfield, when he up and broke jail. He's changed some, all right, but I'm sure it's him."

"It's him, all right. I found a flyer on him in the office."

Wiesmulluer nodded, looking pleased that I

proved him right. "They never saw me, and since I never had my rifle with me, I let them pass. I woulda blowed the lot of them out of the saddle, but I didn't want to take on the whole bunch with just my pistol."

"You done the right thing. That's a rough bunch," I said.

"They are that," Wiesmulluer agreed. "You best be careful. You ain't seen the last of them, not by a long shot."

"I'm thinking that you're right about that. You better watch yourself," I warned.

Wiesmulluer nodded, looking off into the distance. "After dinner, I'm going to try and talk Marie into taking the girls and moving into town for a few days." He looked back at the house, a dry chuckle rising up from his throat. "I don't know if I can talk her into it. I swear, sometimes that woman is balky as a mule." A worried look crossed his face as he glanced back at the house. "It's not that Marie and the girls can't take care of theirselves, 'cause they can, but that Hetfield, he worries me. Part of what they was going to hang him for was attacking a young woman."

"He worries me too," I said. "If you want, I can stick around and help you get them loaded up."

"That's okay, like you said, you need to get back to town. It may take me the rest of the day to talk them into the notion. If I get that done, I can get their junk moved."

"Well, I guess I'll head back to town," I said, taking the reins and swinging aboard my horse.

Wiesmulluer grabbed my bridle, all the friendliness disappearing from his eyes. "Just remember,

I want you to find the man who slaughtered my steer.''

"Yes, sir," I promised, waiting for him to release my horse. The old man gave me a hard look, then nodded and let go of my horse.

Giving him a salute, I wheeled my horse and galloped out of the yard. As soon as I was clear of their yard, I slowed to a trot.

I begin to think about Eddy and Betsy. For the first time, I looked past that dazzling smile and all that yeller hair and saw Betsy for what she was. Now, don't go getting me wrong, Betsy is a fine woman, but she's money hungry.

Eddy, now, she was different. Just thinking of her was enough to set my palms to sweating and my heart to pounding. I kicked myself for not speaking my mind when I had the chance. Pounding my fist against my thigh, I wished I had the nerve to tell her how I felt.

I'd just about ground my teeth down to nubs when I finally reached Whiskey City. The first place I went was to the hotel, namely Phillip Thomas's room. The lawyer wasn't in his room, but he had been there.

I knew that because his stuff was gone, every last bit of it. Pulling the door closed behind me, I hurried down to the desk. I wanted to see if the lawyer had checked out. As I passed Lilly Simmons's room, I heard voices speaking from inside. One of them was a man's voice.

Stopping, I hesitated, then rapped on the door, hoping that Thomas was in Lilly's room. It seemed reasonable to me. They had to know each other, since Thomas had been her husband's lawyer.

"Just a second," Lilly's voice called from behind the closed door, followed by the sound of scuffling feet.

Lilly opened the door just wide enough for her face to peek out. "Good day, Sheriff. Has someone found my mine?" she asked, her face as lovely and composed as ever.

"No, ma'am," I replied, trying to look past her and into the room. "I'm looking for that lawyer, Thomas. I thought he might be here," I said, doing my best to remember Eddy's words of caution about this woman. Just looking at her smiling face, I had a hard time believing that a dishonest thought ever even crossed her mind.

Lilly smiled up at me. "No, Sheriff, I'm here by myself."

"Huh, that's funny. I coulda swore I heard voices."

Lilly laughed, patting her hair. "That was probably me. I have a habit of talking to myself."

Without thinking, I raised up on my toes, looking over her head. What I could see of the room appeared empty, but a man could easily be hiding under the bed or in the closet. Seeing my look, Lilly stepped back a pace, closing the door a little, a hard look coming to her face. "If that's all you needed, I'm very tired."

I hurriedly dropped my eyes back down to her face. "Sure thing, ma'am. I'm sorry to have bothered you."

"No bother at all," Lilly assured me, but her tone was rather cool, and no warmth showed in her face.

I frowned as the door slammed in my face. Maybe Eddy was right about Miss Lilly. I could have sworn I heard a man in that room. Rubbing my jaw, I walked down the stairs.

Mrs. Fowler was behind the desk. She looked up, giving me a tired smile.

"Howdy, Mrs. Fowler. Has that lawyer fella, Thomas, checked out?"

"I don't believe so, but I haven't seen him since he checked in. He paid for two weeks when he signed in."

"Two weeks?" I mused. I figured Thomas would leave Whiskey City as soon as he completed his business. "He must be looking for that map himself."

"I don't know. He didn't tell me his business," Mrs. Fowler said, sounding apologetic because she couldn't help me.

"Thank you, Mrs. Fowler. If you happen to see him, I'd appreciate it if you would tell him that I need to have a word with him."

After I left the hotel, I went through the whole town. I mean, I checked from stem to stern, but Thomas was nowhere to be found. I asked everyone I saw, but no one had seen the little lawyer since Monday. More than a little puzzled, I went down to the livery to have a chat with Mr. Burdett. I found him working at his forge, his face still scratched up.

"Are you here to work?" Burdett asked eagerly. "'Cause my back's been ailin' me something terrible."

"No, sir, I'm looking for Thomas. Have you seen him?"

Burdett set aside the plowshare he was sharpening and scratched his head. "No, come to think of it, I haven't seen him since that afternoon in the saloon."

"Is his horse still here?"

"Naw, he didn't have no horse. He came in on the stage, I reckon."

"He couldn't have," I said, shaking my head. "The stage only comes through on Wednesdays. Thomas showed up on a Monday."

A slow look of wonderment spread across Burdett's wide face. "You know, that's right. Well, I don't know how he got to town, but he never left no horse here."

"He had to. There ain't no other place in town to stable a horse, and he sure didn't come in here on a magic carpet," I argued.

"I don't know anything about that. All I know is that Bobby Stamper came down here and said there was a meeting over at the saloon. By the time I got over there, this Thomas feller was saying how Turley died, and that he wanted us to have a drink to his memory."

"Wait a minute. Stamper told you about the meeting?"

"Yeah, he was rounding everybody up."

Now that was a downright interesting piece of information. Waving absently at Burdett, I left the stable. Walking around town, I done some checking, and no one in town could remember seeing Thomas since he left the saloon right after reading Turley's will. It was as if the man appeared out of thin air and vanished the same way.

I was giving up my search when I realized Bobby Stamper was also missing. I'd been through the town twice, and the outlaw was nowhere to be found.

Chapter Nine

I was bothered. I preferred having Stamper around where I could keep an eye on him. When I couldn't find him, well, I just knew he was up to something. Not that I feared Stamper the way I did Butch and his mob. Stamper might steal every last dollar in town, but I'd take a bet that he wouldn't kill anyone. Butch and Hetfield, now, they were a whole other box of frogs. They'd kill just for the pleasure of it.

I walked down the middle of the street as night claimed the land. Stopping in the middle of the street, I took off my hat, wiping the sweat from my brow. Turning in a circle, I swept the town with my eyes. Like a cold wind, doubt crept up on me. So much was happening, and I wondered if I could handle what I knew was coming.

Blowing out a big sigh, I slapped my hat back on my head. One thing was certain, I couldn't get anything done on an empty stomach. I was heading for the hotel when Joe Havens stuck his head out of the saloon door.

"Teddy! Get over here quick!" he yelled, waving his arms excitedly.

Pulling my pistol, I broke into a run. "It's Wiesmulluer and Claude, they're at it again!" Joe hollered.

Sliding my pistol back in the holster, I pulled to a stop in front of the saloon. I looked through the window and sure enough, Claude and Wiesmulluer were squared off in the middle of the barroom floor, both of them looking happy as pups.

A leering grin on his face, Wiesmulluer battered the smaller Frenchman with a barrage of heavy punches. Claude rocked on rubbery legs and blood flowed freely from a cut over his eye. The crowd, gathered in a circle around the fighters, let out a cheer every time Wiesmulluer landed one of them splattering blows.

Wiesmulluer nailed Claude square on the chin, and for a second I thought the Frenchman was going to cave in. Despite his appearance, Claude was a long ways from being finished. Wiesmulluer was about to find that out. Setting his feet, Wiesmulluer sent a straight right hand crashing into Claude's face. Waving his arms wildly, Claude staggered backward, his back slamming into the bar. Roaring like a bull, Wiesmulluer charged in to finish the job. That was a mistake.

His back braced against the bar, Claude grabbed the bar rail, raised his feet, then drove both heels into Wiesmulluer's face. The old man stopped like he'd run into a brick wall. For a brief moment, he hung on his feet. Then, like a butterfly caught in a heavy rain, he wilted to the floor. He lay there, unmoving, as the cheering sputtered and died away.

For a second, the saloon was quiet as a funeral parlor, as Joe Havens solemnly drew his knife. Standing on tiptoe, he scratched a tally on Claude's side of the board. Grinning back at the crowd, he took down the jar of money.

I felt sorry for poor Mr. Wiesmulluer. Folks stepped right over the top of him as they crowded up to the bar to have a drink and settle up the winnings.

Dropping to one knee, I helped the old man as he struggled to set up. "You all right?" I asked.

"Yeah, I'm fine," the old man grumbled, slapping away my hands as I tried to help him to his feet.

Wiesmulluer sucked in a deep breath, swaying on his feet like a wounded bull. Claude stood at the bar, accepting the winner's spoils, a free drink and a barrelful of backslapping. Claude turned away from the bar, and for a second his eyes met Wiesmulluer's.

They stared at each other for a long moment, and something seemed to pass between them. Abruptly, Wiesmulluer turned away. "I've got to get home," he mumbled, bending over stiffly as he snatched his hat from the floor.

Rubbing his jaw, Wiesmulluer wobbled out the door. Hesitating for just a second, I followed behind him. I hurried to catch up. "I take it you talked your family into moving into town," I said.

"That's right!" the old man snapped, stalking toward his wagon. All of a sudden, he stopped so quick that I durn near ran into him. He turned to face me, a curious expression on his face. "Eddy seems to set store by you," he said slowly.

I felt my face burning red, but I held his gaze. "I reckon I think a lot of her too."

Wiesmulluer nodded. "I can see that." He looked right at me, and I saw that one of his eyes was already swelling shut. "I would take it kindly if you would keep an eye on my family. I don't care for the way things are shaping up. If word about that blasted mine gets out, we'll have half the country breathing down our necks. I've no doubt that some of them that come looking for the mine will be good men, but most of them won't be."

"Don't worry, sir, I won't let anything happen to them. You can count on me."

A ghost of a smile flirted with his bruised lips. "I know I can, son," he said, squeezing my shoulder.

You know something, for the first time I wasn't scared of that old man. Now, it had nothing to do with the fact that he'd just been whupped. It was something in his face.

"Mr. Wiesmulluer, what's with you and Mr. Claude? For as long as I've known you, you two have been fighting. How come you don't make peace?"

Boy, I done it that time. That old man gave me a look that chilled me to the bone. "That wouldn't be any of your concern!" he snapped, turning his back on me. He limped over to his wagon, grunting in pain as he heaved his body up into the seat. I waved at him, but he didn't even look over at me; he just snapped the reins and drove out of town.

Shaking my head, I started back toward the saloon. I don't reckon I'd ever figure out what makes that old bugger tick. Folks were crowded up to the bar, slurping down Joe Havens's whiskey and reliving the fight. Just listening to them, I wondered if them fellers saw the same fight as I did.

"Hey, Sheriff!" Joe shouted, waving a fistful of money in the air. "This is Turley's share of the winnings. What do you reckon we should do with it?"

"It should go to his widow," I decided. "I'm going over to the hotel, I can drop it by to her."

The spirits in the place sank like a rock in the swimming hole. I guess they had planned on splitting the money. Shoving Lilly's money into my pocket, I trudged out of the saloon. A bone-deep weariness settled on my shoulders with a heavy hand. Dragging my feet, I shuffled to the hotel.

Lilly answered the door, smiling immediately. "Sheriff! What a wonderful surprise. Do come in," she said, swinging the door wide. I really didn't want to. I felt like I'd been drug through a gopher hole. Before I could make an excuse, she grabbed me by the arm and pulled me in. She sat down on the bed, looking up at me with them bewitching green eyes. "I'm so glad you came by. I've been thinking about you," she said, patting the bed.

"You have?" I asked, keeping my distance.

"Yes, I have," Lilly said, batting them eyes at me. "I've been thinking, and I'd like to make you a proposition."

"What's that?" I asked, all of a sudden feeling like a fish swimming past a baited hook.

"I know where the map is," she said.

"Where?" I asked, a little breathless.

Lilly smiled, patting my hand. "Not so fast," she said. "Now, I know for a fact that somebody found the map. If you would go find him and take the map, we could split the gold." Lilly looked up at me, batting them eyes again. "Maybe we could go back east together."

She looked pretty as a fresh colt, and was offering me a fortune, but you know, I wasn't even tempted. Well, okay, maybe I was a little tempted, but I shook my head. I'd finally gotten around to figuring out that Eddy was the one for me—now I just had to convince Eddy.

"Miss Lilly, if somebody found the map, then I'm happy for them, and I'll keep my promise to you. I'll see about getting you a share of the gold."

"Share!" Lilly screamed, her face twisting up. "I don't want a lousy share. I want it all!"

"Now, Miss Lilly," I said, hoping to calm her down.

"Get out!" she screamed.

I gladly backed out the door. That woman was crazy as a loco horse. I left her money on the dresser and walked down the hall to my room. One thing about it, Eddy had been right about Lilly.

Yawning, I opened my door. As I started to undress, I heard the rumble of thunder. I crossed to the window. Blowing out my light, I glanced out of the window, watching the approaching storm. As the first drops of rain fell, I saw a man creep out of the back door of the hotel. In the gloom, I saw him inch down the alley, but I couldn't recognize him. Keeping my eyes glued on the shadowy figure, I reached back for my pistol, which I'd draped over the back of the chair.

The man mounted his horse, and as he rode away, lightning flashed. In the brief flash of light, I saw him clearly.

Bobby Stamper!

Chapter Ten

The next morning I woke slowly, my brain fighting through the layers of sleep that lay across my thoughts like a fog. Rolling over in the soft bed, I stretched, fighting the temptation to simply let the fog reclaim me. By sheer willpower I forced myself to set up.

Swinging my legs off the bed, I leaned over and rubbed my face. Fighting off a yawn, I reached for my pants. I dressed slowly, wondering what could go wrong today.

Still more asleep than awake, I stumbled down to the kitchen. Most of the folks already eating looked like I felt. In no mood for company, I took a table in the back and waited for my food. I ate my breakfast without even knowing what it was. Instead of helping me wake up, the meal made me even sleepier. I knew I should get out and about, but I decided to go over to the office and sorta let my meal soak in. Part of the problem was, I didn't know what to do.

Dragging my spurs, I crossed the street to the jail. It was a glorious morning, bright and sunny. The rain had washed the land clean, leaving a bright new feeling behind. Maybe it was a grand morning, but all I could do was wonder how many such mornings like this we had left. Mr. Wiesmulluer was right. Once word of Turley's mine got out, Whiskey City was in for some changes.

Feeling a little wistful, I sat down at the desk, propping my feet up on its scarred surface. Tipping my hat down, I closed my eyes and pondered all that had happened last night. Lilly said someone had found the map; I wondered who, and how Lilly managed to find out about it. To top things off, that crazy Stamper was up to something. I just wish I knew what. Then it hit me: Stamper had found the map!

I was lost in my thoughts when the door crashed open. From the way that door slammed open, I half-expected to look up and see a hurricane bearing down on me. What I saw was a dark-haired, black-eyed tornado.

"Theodore Cooper, you lowdown, four-flushing, double-dealing coyote!" Eddy Wiesmulluer screamed, slamming the door shut with enough force to rock the whole building.

For a second, I didn't know what to do, then I started to ask what I'd done this time. That was a mistake; I shoulda dove down behind the desk for cover.

Eddy grabbed a box of rifle shells from the shelf by the door. Drawing all the way back, she hurled them right at me. I saw them streaking at me, but with my feet still propped up on the desk, I wasn't at all in a good position to react. I tried to pull my feet in and catch the shells all at the same time. In my haste and confusion, I did neither.

That box of shells clobbered me right on the cheekbone, the impact knocking my chair over. Bellowing loudly, I crashed to the floor. On my hands and knees, I shook my head, trying to clear the cobwebs. Then I started to get mad. What in blue blazes had got into that fool woman this time?

I raised up from behind the desk, fully intending to let her have a piece of my mind. Now, Eddy musta been just waiting for me to raise my head, cause my eyes barely cleared the top of the desk before a box of shotgun shells clobbered me in the forehead, followed real close by a box of pistol cartridges.

The next few minutes I was a right busy man, doing my best to duck the boxes that came flying at me and covering up my tender areas when I couldn't dodge fast enough. Let me tell you, for a small mite of a girl, Eddy could fling them shells with a lotta force and uncanny accuracy.

"I should have known better than to trust a coyote like you!" Eddy screamed, throwing the last box. At last, she was out of bullets.

Thinking the danger was over, I came out from behind the desk. "I don't know what's put the bees in your britches, but can't we talk this over?" I pleaded.

Eddy's eyes flashed and narrowed down to slits. "Don't you play dumb with me, Theodore Cooper," she warned, a dangerous tint in her voice.

I had to scratch my head over that one. Maybe I was dumb, cause I sure wasn't playacting. I didn't have the foggiest notion what she was blabbering about.

"I   heard   all   about   you   and   that . . . that

woman!'' Eddy screamed, and before I knew it she grabbed up the broom and splattered me full in the face with it. Sputtering and coughing, I spat out dust and pieces of straw while I pawed at the cobwebs on my face. ''What did you go and do that for?'' I roared, starting to get downright mad. I mean, a man can only take so much, and I was just about to get a bellyful.

For an answer, Eddy hauled off and pasted me again with that dang broom. ''Don't you try and deny it. Betsy saw you coming out of Lilly Simmons' room last night. I swear, I don't know what you see in her. She's nothing but a harlot.''

''Aw, come on, Eddy, we weren't doing nothing. I had to go see her on law business. I had some money to give her.''

''I bet!'' Eddy said, and for a second I thought she would give me one last whack with the broom. Instead, she threw the broom to the floor, a dangerous look flashing in her eyes. ''Don't lie to me,'' she hissed.

More than a little taken a back by the emotion in her voice, I took a long step back, trying to judge her reach. ''Honest, Eddy, I had some stuff for her, that's all.''

Eddy didn't bother answering, she just kicked the broom at me and stomped out the door. For a long time I didn't move, I just stood there staring at the door, my stomach feeling like I'd just been kicked.

I don't know how long I stood there, but when I went to fetch my horse, my steps were slow and heavy. Trying to push Eddy from my mind and concentrate on business, I slapped my saddle on my horse.

I didn't ride toward the nest of rocks behind Turley's dugout, even though that was my destination. Instead, I rode out in the other direction, figuring to circle around and slip up on the place from behind.

As I rode, an anger welled up inside me. That dang Eddy! She had no call to be angry with me. No sir, no reason at all. I hadn't done anything wrong. I had to say one thing for her, once that girl got a notion in her head, there was no getting rid of it.

I rode until I was out of sight from town, then turned my horse off the trail, working in a giant arc. As I rode, I kept my eyes peeled for any sign of Butch and his men or their camp. That's when I saw the body jammed in the rocks.

I reckon if I hadn't been looking so hard for a sign, I woulda likely rode right past it none the wiser. All that was visible was an outflung hand and part of one leg.

When I spotted the body, I sawed back on the reins hard enough to make my horse throw his head and dance sideways. While he settled down, my eyes swept the country and my hand fingered my rifle. All looked quiet, no danger presenting itself. Not trusting appearances, I slowly slid my rifle from the boot. Glancing around again, I dried my palms on my shirt, not liking this one bit.

Dropping the reins, I slid from the saddle and slowly approached the body. Crouching down, I scanned the ground. After the rain, no tracks were on the ground. I stopped, sweeping the area with my eyes. Nothing moved, and I was starting to feel a little foolish. Nonetheless, I eased carefully up to the body.

As I knelt beside the dead man, I took one last long look around, then turned my attention to the body. I let out a low whistle when I saw his face. My fears forgotten, I leaned my rifle against a rock. No sooner did I let go of my gun than I heard the chilling sound of a pistol being cocked behind me.

For a long second, not a sound could be heard, not even the sound of a restless wind stirring. Even my own heart stopped beating as I tensed my muscles, straining my ears. A lone bead of sweat trickled down my face with agonizing slowness.

"Stand up and turn around," a familiar sounding voice said. Now, maybe that voice sounded familiar, but that did little to cheer my bones. Let me tell you, that gent's voice sounded 'bout as friendly as the buzz of a rattler. For a second I looked at my rifle. If I could snatch it and roll behind them rocks . . .

"Don't even think about making a try for that popgun. You'd never make it," the man said coldly.

Something about his cool tone convinced me. Holding my hands away from my body, I stood up and turned around. My blood ran cold as I recognized the man behind the pistol. All of a sudden, me knees felt slack and a shiver raced up and down my spine.

Chapter Eleven

"What's the matter, boy? You look like you just seen a ghost."

"You're supposed to be dead," I whispered.

A loud, cackling laugh gushed out of his mouth, startling me and grating on my jangled nerves. Dropping his pistol into the holster, he laughed again, slapping his thigh. "You should see your face," he said, wiping a tear from his eye.

"Turley Simmons, you crazy old goat, you're supposed to be dead!" I shouted, starting to get good and mad.

Turley chuckled, shaking his head. "Maybe, I am. Maybe I'm a spook," he said gleefully. "Shoot, boy, do I look dead to you?"

"What are you doing way out here? You crazy coot, you like to have scared me plumb to death," I roared.

"I reckon I did at that," Turley agreed, still hehawing. "You shoulda seen your shoulders hump up when I cocked ol' Bessie here," he said, slapping his pistol.

I snatched up my own rifle, angling the business end at him. "I got half a mind to haul you into jail," I threatened between clenched teeth.

Turley chuckled, in no way intimidated by the rifle. "Well, you was half-right, anyway. I'd say you got about half a mind."

"I ain't fooling," I told him. "You keep it up and you'll find yourself setting in a cell in town."

"I ain't foolin'" Turley mimicked, making a face at me. "What did I do?" he asked, sounding mighty innocent.

"How about imitating a dead man," I growled, feeling surly as an old bear. "I suppose that map is just another one of your fool pranks?"

Grinning, Turley spat on the ground. "No, the map is real enough, and anybody that finds it can have it." Turley laughed, shaking his head.

"We'll know soon enough," I told him. "Somebody went and found the map."

Turley's face split wide open with a grin and he laughed gleefully. "You mean Bobby Stamper?" he asked, cackling louder with each word. "He sure thinks he found the map, but he's in for a foolin'."

"What do you mean?" I asked.

"I saw him snooping around the well at my cabin. He peered down the well for a long time, then hot-footed it into town. After he left, I made a fake map and hid it in the well. Before long, he came hotfootin' it back with a rope." Turley laughed, shaking his head. "You shoulda seen him dancing around. No sir, Stamper never found the map. Like I said, I hid that map real good. It ain't gonna be easy to find.''

"You can say that again," I grumbled. "The whole town has nearly went crazy looking and nobody's found it yet."

Setting my rifle down again, I turned my back on Turley and went to prying the dead man out of the rocks. "You want to give me a hand? He's jammed in here pretty good," I said, struggling to lift the dead man.

Grunting, Turley wedged his body up beside mine. "Galloping garterbelts, that's that lawyer feller, Thomas!" he exclaimed. "Now, who in the devil would want to kill him?"

"If I knew that, I'd go arrest the jasper," I said irritably. "You gonna stand there gawking all day, or give me a hand?"

Turley bent down to help me. "I declare, you sure have gotten to be a fire-eater, ever since they pinned that star on your shirt." Turley shook his head mournfully. "I never seen it to fail, give a man a little authority and it goes right to his head."

"Shut up," I growled. I'd took about all the lip from Turley that I meant to.

Together, we pulled Thomas from the rocks and laid him out on the sand. Looking him over, I saw that he'd been shot twice in the chest from real close. Close enough to scorch his shirt a mite. While I looked at the body, Turley leaned in close, almost touching my face with his. "Dang, boy, what happened to your face? You look like you been drug through a keyhole."

"Shut up!" I snapped. "Where's your horse?"

Turley grinned, his crooked teeth flashing.

"What makes you so certain that I have a horse?" he asked slyly.

Now, before, I'd always liked Turley, but I was just starting to see what a royal pain in the backside he could be. Pulling my pistol, I jabbed him in the gizzard. "You can walk all the way to town. Makes no difference to me," I snarled.

"I weren't figuring on going in to town," Turley said, crossing his arms and getting stubborn on me.

"I don't recall asking if you wanted to go into town," I snapped, my patience thin as boarding-house soup. "You're under arrest!"

"Arrest?" Turley howled. "Why in blue blazes would you want to go and arrest me for?" he asked, sounding like a coon dog with his foot in a trap.

"How about for killing him?" I said, pointing to Thomas.

Turley snorted, spitting on the ground. He cocked his head off to one side, looking at me closely. "What in tarnation are you using for brains, sawdust? I didn't kill him. Shoot, I just got here. I didn't even know he was dead."

"How come you're here? I s'pose you just happened along."

Turley squatted down on his heels, mocking me with his smile. "I was follering you." He chuckled, shaking his head. "You're getting to be pretty smart. Maybe too smart for your own good." Turley squinted. "I seen where you'd been snooping around my camp. I knew you'd be back, so I been keeping my eye on you."

"So that was you watching the town!"

"Sure was, and lordy, did I ever see an eyeful. I durn near busted a seam when Andrews bent that stovepipe over Joe's head. When all that soot plastered Iris in the face, I figured she'd hit the roof.''

Before I even knew what was happening, I found myself laughing right with the old goat. Realizing what he was up to, I snapped my jaws shut and whacked him across the head and shoulders with my hat. "Don't try that with me; it ain't gonna work!" I said, giving him another whack.

"Try what?" Turley asked, waving the dust away from his face.

"Getting me off the track," I said, giving him a stern look. "You're going to jail and that's final."

Turley swore, turning away. "Teddy, you got no call to treat me thisaway. Jumping juniper beans, I'll miss all the fun sitting in that jail."

"Maybe, but the way I see it, Thomas musta been killed by somebody he knew and trusted," I said, pointing to the bullet holes, which had obviously been fired from point-blank range. "And you are the only person in town who really knew Thomas."

Turley jerked his hat off and threw it on the ground. He swore viciously as he kicked his hat. "Teddy, I swear, you ain't got no more brains than a short pup. Why in the world would I want to kill Thomas?"

"I don't know, but somebody killed him, and right now, you seem like the most likely suspect." Now, I never really believed Turley killed the lawyer, but I wanted to get him into town and that seemed like a handy excuse. I had a feeling that the people in town could pry out the location of the map and this whole mess would be over.

"Come on, Teddy, you know'd me all your life. You know I wouldn't kill anybody. Well, not unless they were cheatin' at cards or something like that,'' Turley said, changing from being mad to pleading. ''Thomas was a shyster, but that's what I liked about him. I didn't snuff him, and you got no reason to take me in.''

''Well, how about butchering that steer of Wiesmulluer's?'' I countered, feeling mighty smug.

I figured Turley would argue and deny the fact until his dying day, but instead he grinned broadly, managing to look almost proud of himself. ''You found out about that, did ye?''

''I sure did. Wiesmulluer bellowed like a cow stuck in the mud when he seen it,'' I said as Turley slapped his knee and cackled.

Turley scratched the stubble on his chin. ''I figured he'd go straight over to Claude's, but he never done it,'' Turley said, his laughter dying away. ''I sure was disappointed. I was all primed to see them tangle.''

''Let's get going,'' I said, motioning with my pistol.

Turley shifted his feet and crossed his arms. ''I ain't gonna do it,'' he said through clenched teeth. ''And you can't make me.''

Now, there's been times in my life when I wished that I wasn't so dang big, but there's times when it comes in right handy. Just like now.

Instead of arguing with Turley, who I knew could be mule stubborn when he set his mind to it, I just picked the crazy devil up and pitched him across the saddle of my horse.

''You can ride into town like that or you can tell me where your horse is, makes no difference to me.''

Turley grunted and cussed, and tried to set up, but every time he did, I slammed him back down.

"All right, my horse is just around the bend," he said finally.

"That's better," I said, dragging him off the horse by the scruff of his neck.

Turley staggered back a couple of steps, then fell, skidding across the ground on the seat of his britches. "I still say you got no call to treat me like this. I ain't done nothing," Turley bawled.

"You just owned up to a crime," I reminded him.

"Huh?" Turley said, scratching his head. "What in dangnation are you blabbing about?"

"Killing Wiesmulluer's steer," I said curtly.

Turley snorted loudly, cutting his eyes to the sky. "Heck, tormenting Wiesmulluer ain't a crime; it's a pleasure."

I was of a mind to agree with him, but seeing's how I was the law, I couldn't. "Don't worry about that; just load Thomas on my horse," I ordered.

"Dadgum, overgrown, snot-nosed brat," Turley mumbled under his breath while he boosted Thomas's body up on my horse.

Once he had the body in place, I swung up behind it. I couldn't sit in the saddle right, and my feet didn't reach the stirrups, but it wasn't far back to town, so I figured I could make out. "Let's go get your horse," I said, keeping my rifle trained on Turley.

Turley led off, mumbling under his breath. I swear, he cussed and fumed all the way back to town. Paying him no mind, I rode along, trying to piece together what just happened. Why would anyone want to kill Thomas? I didn't have an answer to that one, but I would bet that it had something to do with that fool map.

We rode into town slowly, and you could hear necks snapping as we rode by. Now, if I'd been riding a two-headed horse, I couldn't have started a bigger stir than I did. Folks dropped what they were doing to stare at us, their jaws hanging plumb down to their boot tops.

Turley rocked in the saddle, laughing gleefully and pounding his thigh. "Look at 'em, Teddy. Why, a body would think they never saw a corpse jump up out of the boneyard and ride through town before!"

"Never mind that. Just head over to the jail," I ordered.

Turley's good humor evaporated like a drop of water on a hot rock. He sputtered and complained, but I paid that no mind. I just kept herding him until he was inside the sheriff's office.

"Dang, Teddy," he muttered, his eyes sweeping the room. "It wouldn't kill you to drag a broom across the floor every once in a while."

"Shut up and get in the cell," I said with a growl, helping him along with he sole of my boot. As he skidded across the floor of the cell, I slammed the barred door shut. "Maybe some time in the pokey will learn you not to get everybody all riled up with your fool pranks."

Turley made a face at me, but I ignored him as I turned the key in the lock. I was just putting the key in the desk, when most of the town crowded into my office. I swear, there was so many folks wedged in there, that place was bustin' at the seams.

They all tried to talk at once, but Iris Winkler's squawky crooning drowned the rest out. "Turley

Simmons, you're supposed to be dead!'' she said, pointing a bony finger at him.

Turley bent over at the waist, cackling loudly. ''Iris, you old biddy! How the heck you been?'' Turley danced a jig around the cell. ''Do I look dead to you?''

Now, even on her best day, Iris ain't exactly what you'd call a patient woman, and Turley's laughter and mocking smile was more than enough to set her off. Dark color shot to her face, and she clenched her fists, going off like a basket of blasting powder. ''You're gonna be dead quick enough,'' she yelled, taking a swipe at him through the bars.

Her punch missed by a good three feet as Turley backed away. ''Sheriff! Sheriff!'' he yelled, putting a hand to his face. ''Help me, please!'' he screamed, then let out a snicker.

''You're lucky I don't help her,'' I threatened. ''Now shut up 'fore I give her the key.''

''Shoot, I declare, this whole town has turned into a bunch of soreheads,'' Turley complained disgustedly.

''Well, what do you expect? You got the whole town in a tizzy over the phony gold mine,'' Andrews said, sounding like he just lost a loved one.

Turley grinned, cocking one eyebrow slyly. ''Who said there was no mine?''

The jail went silent as a tomb as the whole bunch sucked in a deep breath and held it. Andrews clasped his hands in front of him, almost falling to his knees. ''Well, is there a mine or not?'' he asked, his voice pleading.

''Sure, there's a mine. The map wouldn't be any good if there wasn't,'' Turley said, sporting a wide grin.

In a heartbeat, smiles wiped out the angry looks. "Where's the map?" Blanche Caster demanded, gripping the bars of the cell.

"It's hid," Turley said, sounding right proud of himself. "But whoever finds the map can have the mine."

Blanche jerked on the bars, pressing her face up against them. "I asked you where the map was, buster!" she snapped. "Now, fess up, before I take a willow switch to your hind end."

Turley backed up, sitting down on the cot. He folded his arms and crossed his legs. "I ain't telling."

Grinding her teeth, Blanche shook the bars hard enough to rattle the whole building. Like a pack of wild dogs closing in for the kill, the rest of the folks surged up to the bars, growling and snapping.

They didn't faze Turley in the least. He merely smiled, sitting on his bunk. He clasped his hands on his knees and rocked back and forth, looking like the cat that ate the canary.

"If you want the mine, you'll just have to find the map," he told them calmly. "But enough about that, I want to know what's been going on in town. Iris, how's that chimney I built for you working out? Does it draw well? I wasn't sure it would."

For a second, nobody moved and nobody spoke. Then somebody broke for the door. Like a stampede, one person moved and that set the rest off. They hit the door running out. The only problem was that the door was built with one person in mind, and they all hit it at the same time.

Grunting and cussing, they strained to get through. Now, ol' Andrews might be a soft, chubby-looking gent, but he clawed through first. He seemed to squirt through the door, then fell into the street. Once Andrews made it through, the rest popped out and were off.

Turley let out a high-pitched squeal, grabbing the bars and jumping up and down. "Look at 'em go," he howled. "Come on, Teddy, let me out so I can see the fun," he pleaded, still jumping up and down.

"Is the map in the chimney?"

Turley snorted. "Course not. That's too easy. Now spring me, so I can see the fun."

"Where's the map?" I asked.

"I ain't telling," Turley said.

"Have it your way. Don't fret. I'll tell you all about it," I said, moving toward the door.

Turley yelped, kicking the bars. Ignoring his howling and cussing, I walked out the door, mighty proud of myself for showing the old-timer who was in charge. One thing about it, I was going to teach him some respect for the law.

By the time I reached Iris's house, it looked like an ant den that'd been kicked over. Folks swarmed around it, trying to find a way up on the roof.

Andrews had already made it onto the roof and had wrapped both arms around the chimney, hugging it for dear life. Slipping and sliding on the slick wooden shingles, Iris closed in on him. Screeching like a mad chicken, she grabbed Andrews by the ears and hauled back.

Despite Iris's best efforts, Andrews remained clamped on to that chimney like a snapping turtle. Joe Havens was the next to reach the chimney. He took a different approach from Iris. Jerking his pistol, he hammered Andrews' pudgy fingers with the butt.

Their combined efforts done the trick. Andrews' fingers popped loose and he and Iris flipped over backward. Andrews rolled off the roof and landed on the water barrel. Iris rolled halfway down the roof, skidding to a stop with her legs poking up in the air.

Having the chimney to himself for a moment, Joe rammed his gun in his britches and went to clawing and scratching at the chimney. Cussing, he kicked it several times, but nothing happened. I reckon ol' Joe was gettin' desperate, 'cause he hauled out his pistol and let 'er pop.

Poking out his tongue, Joe ripped off a couple of more shots. Them bullets bounced off that chimney screaming like banshees. Gid had been closing in when the shots rang out. As the bullets whined past his head, Gid done a belly flop and disappeared. It sounded like a clap of thunder as shingles flew in the air and Gid ripped through the roof.

Instinctively I dove for the ground at the sound of gunfire. As I climbed back to my feet, a hooting laugh assaulted my ears. Glancing over my shoulder, I saw Turley sitting on a bale of hay and holding a bottle of whiskey.

Rocking back and forth, he pounded his knee. "Gawd almighty!" he roared. "This is better than one of them shows in Kansas City," he cackled, holding the bottle up to his mouth.

"How'd you get here? I locked you in the jail!"

"It didn't take," Turley said, chuckling. He helped himself to a big snort. "Shoot, boy, I got away from a whole camp full of Blackfeet one time. Getting out of that jail was easy."

"Well, don't you fret, 'cause you're going right back," I said, seething on the inside.

My words had no effect on Turley. He simple helped himself to another pull from his bottle. "You stay right here," I told him as I watched

Burdett crawling up on the house totting a sledge-hammer.

Before I could decide whether or not it was my place to stop him, Burdett lit into that chimney. It didn't take him long to smash that chimney into a pile of mortar and rocks. Them folks combed through the debris, but just like Turley predicted, they never found any map.

As soon as they were sure Turley never cemented the map into the chimney, the crowd began to get ugly and cast mean looks in Turley's direction. Growling and snapping like wild dogs, they closed in.

Chapter Twelve

I figured I'd best get Turley locked back up for his own good. The way the crowd was acting, they were liable to lynch him. Not that I could really blame them.

My paws latched onto Turley's neck, I drug him kicking and screaming back to the jail. Tossing him in the cell, I double-checked the lock to make sure it was shut tight. I was just finishing when Iris stormed in, blowing and snorting like a typhoon. "Did you see what they done to my house," she raved, practically frothing at the mouth.

"Yeah, I seen it," I replied warily.

"Well, what are you going to do about it?" Iris demanded, placing her hands on her hips.

"I don't rightly know," I said slowly.

"You don't know!" Iris screamed. "You are supposed to be the sheriff of this town. You're supposed to protect the property of the citizens. Those people wrecked my house!"

"Seemed to me like you had a hand in it," I

said, shooting a mean look at Turley when he snickered. "Besides, what happened to your house ain't no worse than what you and Gid done to Mr. Andrews' bank," I pointed out as Turley howled and danced around the cell.

Now that put a hitch in Iris's getalong, but it never stopped her. "Well, somebody is going to pay for fixing my house, even if it has to be you,"she threatened.

Having spoken her piece, Iris started to leave. Her eyes roamed over the shells and papers everywhere on the floor. "Teddy, clean this pigsty up; it's a disgrace." With that, she flung her dress around and stomped out the door. As the door slammed behind her, I blew out a big breath. "Ol' Iris sure was on the prod," Turley said, taking a big pull from his bottle and smacking his lips. "What you planning to do about her shack? You better do something or she'll hound you the rest of your days."

"Shut up," I growled, pacing my small office. "This is all your fault. You had to mention that chimney," I hissed.

"Fun though, wasn't it?" Turley said, grinning around the neck of his bottle.

"Not for me it wasn't," I snapped.

"Aw, cheer up. Here, have a belt, things will look better tomorrow," Turley said, holding out the bottle. "A few snorts of this will chase your troubles away."

"I don't want to cheer up and I don't want a drink," I thundered. Glaring at the old trapper, I approached the bars. "What I want is for you to tell me where the map is."

Turley took a small sip, eyeing me critically over the bottle. "So the bug has bit you too. You've

been thinking about all that gold,'' he said accusingly.

''No, I don't care about that. I just want things
to get back to normal,'' I said, too frazzled to hold
my anger very long.

''Come on now, fess up. You got a hankering
for that gold just like the others. Why, just think
of it, you could go to one of them cities and have
all them pretty women chasing after you.''

''It seems to me that if a man had that mine,
mostly he'd have one big headache. He wouldn't
have time for all that parading around town. He'd
either be digging or guarding what he already dug.
No, sir, I don't want no part of that mine. All I
want is to save enough money to buy my folks'
place back.''

''What about all them city girls?'' Turley asked,
sporting a sly grin. ''Wouldn't you like to have all
them pretty girls after you?''

''No,''I said, and believe me, I meant it. I mean,
there was only three available girls in this whole
town, and they had me so confused that I didn't
know which way was up. I reckon a whole city full
of them would drive me plumb loco.

''Maybe you already got a girl?'' Turley ven-
tured, a leering smile plastered all over his face.

I looked away, feeling my face turn red and my
ears burn.''No,'' I said, feeling plumb miserable
about it. ''I mean, I don't know. There's this girl
that I like a lot, but she's always mad at me. I don't
reckon she likes me much.''

Turley laughed. ''Boy, you sure don't know
much about women, do you?''

I sighed, looking at the mess in the office. ''I
don't reckon.''

"The girl that's always mad with you, she got a name?"

"Eddy Wiesmulluer."

Turley whistled softly, cocking his head and looking at me like he was seeing me for the first time. "You're a braver man than I figured. That old man catches you chasin' after her and he'll brand your backside with the imprint of his boot."

"I don't guess that it matters much. Like I said, she's mad at me," I groaned. "Just look at what she done to the office."

Turley's eyebrows shot up as he looked at the mess and nodded in appreciation. "That little snip of a gal done all this. Lordy, she must have her ma's temper."

"Her pa's, you mean," I corrected.

Turley snorted, shooting me a disgusted look. "No, I mean her ma's. Now, that old man may be meaner'n a box of snakes, but let me tell you, when that woman of his gets her dander up, ol' Wiesmulluer gets real small, real quick."

"Aw, what does it matter? Eddy doesn't want anything to do with me," I said miserably.

Turley cocked his head, looking at me like I was crazy. "I'm going to give you some advice," he said. "Now, when that little filly flies off the handle at you, that just means that she likes you. What you gotta do is show her who's boss."

"You really think so? It's been my experience that when a body smacks you over the head with a box of cartridges that they aren't happy with you," I said doubtfully.

"Shoot, boy, what do you know? You ain't got no experience in such matters," Turley said, waving off my protests. "Now, the next time Eddy twists off on you, you just give it right back to her with both barrels.''

I scratched my head, thinking it over. Turley's advice surely didn't make much sense to me, but like he said, what did I know.

Turley came to the bars, shaking his head. ''A woman's like a mean horse, you got to show her who's boss. When you argue back, she'll know that you care about her and that you ain't about to stand for a lot of guff.''

''I don't know,'' I said slowly.

''Believe me, you show her who wears the britches and you'll both be happy.''

Before I could make up my mind, Lilly breezed into the office. She favored me with a smile, then shot Turley a hard look. Hands on hips, she glared through the bars at him. ''Turley Simmons, you've worried the life out of me. Here, I thought you was dead.''

''Ain't none of your concern what I do.'' Turley told her.

Lilly's shoulders sagged, and she gave me a tired-looking smile. ''Sheriff, could I talk to my husband in private?''

''Sure, I guess so,'' I replied, picking up my hat. ''Just don't try to break him out,'' I added as I stepped out the door.

I looked back through the window as Lilly approached the bars. Maybe Turley had a point. Lilly came in ready to eat him hide and all, but he bucked right up to her and that seemed to settle her down.

It began to look to me that maybe Turley knew something I didn't. I mean, he'd sure enough landed a right handsome wife. Right then and there,

I made up my mind to take his advice. I'd find Eddy and set her straight.

Mr. Burdett and Mr. Havens were standing out front of the saloon, shooting the breeze. "Have you fellers seen Eddy?" I asked.

They exchanged a look, smiles on their faces. "She's over at the store. Gid hired her to do some picking up around the place," Joe Havens told me.

Thanking them, I hitched up my britches and marched right over to the store. While I walked, I ran through my mind what I was gonna say. Turley was right, Eddy was like a horse. Once I showed her who was running things we'd get along just fine.

Stopping in front of the store, I looked through the window. I could see her inside, running a broom. Right then, I durn near wilted. She looked so pretty. I almost gave in, but then I jerked my hat down and stepped inside.

Eddy looked up, frowning when she saw it was me. "What do you want?" she asked, her voice a mite strained.

"I wanted to talk to you," I said, drawing in a deep breath, then launched into my speech.

I allowed as how I never cared for the way she'd gotten mad and lit into me like I was a mongrel dog. I told her that the only reason I went to Lilly's room was to give her the money.

As I talked, I saw the color rushing up her neck and spreading across her face. I reckon she was embarrassed about the mean way she treated me.

"I sure don't like the way you get all mad, then won't tell me why. And another thing . . . " All of a sudden, my words clogged and stuck in my craw as my throat seized up like a rusty pump.

Eddy had been looking down at the floor, but

when she raised her head, the look on her face liked to have scared the life outta me. Looking in her eyes was like peering down in one of them volcanoes I'd heard about. Her face looked like a powder keg with the fuse lit.

Feeling my hair turning white, I eased back a step. All of a sudden, those black eyes blazed fire and the powder keg went off. Swiping the broomstick under my nose, Eddy marched at me. "Theodore Cooper, if you think you can talk to me like that, you've got another thing coming!"

She stopped, and I blew out a big sigh, thinking the worst was over. Mercy, was I ever wrong. Eddy wasn't near done. In fact, she was just getting started.

Cussing like a muleskinner flogging his team up a steep grade, Eddy commenced to flailing at me with that broom. Covering my head with my arms, I scrambled backward, trying desperately to escape her wrath. All of a sudden my heels hit something hard and stopped. Waving my arms in the air, I fought for balance. I reckon I mighta caught my balance, but Eddy hauled off and thumped me in the chest. Tipping over backward, I fell through the plate-glass window, landing flat on my back. Eddy stepped up to me, pointing that broom handle down at me like it was a lightning rod or something. "Theodore Cooper, I don't ever want to speak to you again!"

As I crawled away like a whipped dog, my ears were assaulted by that familiar hooting laugh. "Lordy, boy, you are dense. Criminy, I think you would fall for anything," Turley said, sporting a fresh bottle of whiskey.

Becoming more than a little tired of this game, I tucked Turley under my arm and drug him back to the jail. I thought about taking the bottle away from him, but decided to let him keep it. Maybe the old coot would get drunk and pass out.

"Turley Simmons, you get out of this cell one more time and I'm gonna bend a rifle barrel over your noggin," I threatened.

Turley's laughter ringing in my ears, I stomped outside. Gathering the reins to my horse, I rode out to the cemetery. I was just finishing planting Thomas, when Stamper and Mr. Wiesmulluer rode up.

"Who you burying?" Wiesmulluer asked.

"That lawyer feller, Thomas," I answered, watching Stamper's reaction.

Stamper didn't show any signs of guilt, not that I could see, anyway. In fact, he smiled. "Looks like we showed up at just the right time," Stamper said.

Stamper's grin and words got under my skin, and I couldn't resist a jab. "I heard you found the map. How much gold did you get?"

Stamper's face turned beet red. Then he swore quickly. Whatever else he might have said was drowned out by a barrage of gunfire coming from town.

Chapter Thirteen

The street in town looked like a battleground: bodies lying about everywhere. Mr. Claude was on his feet, but he staggered around, looking like a drunk show pony. Blood streamed from a big cut over his eye, and a purple bruise already marked his forehead.

Mr. Burdett sat with his back against the saloon, blood flowing from the bullet hole in his leg. Joe Havens lay stretched out flat in the middle of the street with Andrews and Gid standing over him.

Jumping off my horse, I ran over to them. "What happened?" I yelled, grabbing Andrews by the arm and spinning him around.

Gid looked up from working on Joe, a haunted look in his eyes. "It was Butch and his gang. They took Turley out of the jail." Gid glanced at Andrews. "We tried to stop them," he whispered, shifting his gaze to the ground.

"I can see that," I said, patting him on the shoulder. "How's Mr. Havens? Is he going to make it?"

"He's still alive," Andrews said grimly.

Gid stood up, wiping his hands on his jeans. He tried to look at us, but couldn't quite manage it. "They took Eddy and Betsy," his voice a hoarse whisper.

It took a second for his words to sink in, and when they did, they hit me with the force of a run-away train. Feeling like I'd been run over by a stampede, I could only stare in the direction Butch's men took off.

Cursing, Stamper pulled his pistol. He grimly checked the loads, slipping in a shell to bring the weapon up to capacity. His face cold as an approaching storm, he dropped the gun in the holster and pulled a spare from behind his back.

Wiesmulluer didn't move for a long time. Clenching his rough fists, the old man finally found his voice. "They took my girls?" he croaked, sounding lost.

"Be sure and loosen the thong on that pistol, Teddy," Stamper said, walking to his horse. He stopped, looking back at me. "If you got a spare, you might want to fetch it."

I hesitated, not sure what I should do. Gid stepped up, slipping his arm around my shoulders. "You go ahead and find them girls. We'll take care of things here," Gid said, reading my mind.

"I'm going over to the office. We'll be leaving in two minutes," I told Stamper. I started walking to the jail, picking up speed with each step. By the time I reached the door, I was running all out. I threw open the door, banging it off the wall hard enough to break the glass. Ignoring that, I crossed to the desk, jerking open the drawer. From the bottom of the drawer, I pulled a pistol.

I held it for a minute, liking the cool smoothness of the metal. I stared at it for a second, then flipped open the cylinder. Scraping around on the floor, I found enough shells to load the weapon, and an extra handful of bullets which I shoved in my pocket. Once the gun was loaded, I put it behind my back as I saw Stamper do. Jerking my hat down, I strode purposely from the office.

Stamper and Mr. Wiesmulluer sat on their horses, waiting on me. "All right, let's go," I said, feeling tight inside.

Mr. Claude staggered up, leading his horse. "I'm coming with you," he said, holding a rag to his bleeding head.

"You're in no shape for this," Stamper said roughly.

"I'm going," Claude repeated, his voice like granite. He looked across at Wiesmulluer. "I want to help," he said quietly.

Stamper started to object, but Wiesmulluer cut him off. "He's coming," Wiesmulluer said evenly.

Stamper looked to me for support, but I didn't want to argue about it. If Mr. Claude wanted to come, that was fine with me. I had a feeling we might need all the help we could get before this was over.

We rode slowly out of town, four grim men with jaws set firm. I glanced at the others out of the corner of my eye, wondering if they felt the tension like I did. A ball of ice rested heavily in my belly, and my chest felt as if a steel band encircled it. My breathing was shallow, and my heart raced. Doubts began to creep into my mind. Was I equipped to handle men like Hetfield and Butch?

Hetfield! Just the thought of him sent a burst of terror racing through me. Shivering slightly, I rubbed my palms on my thighs. Quickly I glanced around to see if anyone noticed that I was scared, but their attention was focused on the trail, as mine should have been.

I couldn't help it, Hetfield scared me. Then I thought of Eddy in the clutches of a man like Hetfield. All of a sudden, it really hit me. They had Eddy!

My fear melted away as a hot anger claimed me. If they so much as harmed her . . . I didn't finish the thought, I couldn't bear to think about them hurting Eddy.

We rode steadily for two hours, gaining on them every step of the way. We were coming up on a canyon, when we heard voices. Tying the horses, we snuck up to the canyon on foot. Lying on our belies, we gazed over the lip of the canyon.

In the bottom of the canyon, next to a pool of water, was a camp of sorts. Eddy and Betsy sat against the wall of the canyon. They weren't tied, but Red guarded them closely.

Lilly and the rest of the men were grouped in front of Turley. His hands tied behind his back, Turley sat on a rock next to the water. Even from where I lay, I could see a trickle of blood running down his face.

Lilly stood directly in front of him, her hands on her hips, glaring down at him. Right now, Miss Lilly didn't look so pretty, her face twisted and hard. She asked Turley about the map, slapping him when he didn't answer.

"I'll make him talk," Hetfield said, toying with

his knife. In the stillness, his words carried up to us, even though he spoke quietly.

"We're gonna have to do something and do it quick," Wiesmulluer whispered.

I gave a hand signal, and we eased back from the edge. "Anybody got any ideas?" I asked, hoping someone could think of something, because I didn't have any ideas.

"There's four of them and four of us. We could each take a man and pick him off from up here," Mr. Claude suggested.

"No, I doubt if we could ever get a clear shot at all four of them at the same time. Besides, there's too much of a chance of hitting Turley or one of the girls," I said, shaking my head.

"And don't go forgetting about Lilly," Stamper put in. "Don't be fooled by her looks: she's one hard woman."

"How do you know this? Mr. Claude asked, rubbing his hands on the front of his jacket.

Stamper looked up at Claude and grinned slyly. "I knew her in Kansas City." Stamper's grin widened and he waggled his eyebrows. "Believe me, she's no angel."

"Well, what are we going to do? We can't just stand here jawing all day," Wiesmulluer said, his rough veneer starting to crack.

"Me and Bobby will try to slip in closer. You and Mr. Claude can cover us from up here," I decided. "If anything starts, do what you have to do and don't worry about us."

I thought Wiesmulluer was going to argue, but he spun around and crossed to the horses, pulling his and Claude's rifle from the boots.

"Don't worry, Karl. We are going to get them girls back," Claude promised, his voice husky.

For a second, the two old-timers stared at each other. "Thanks," Wiesmulluer said simply. He handed a rifle to Mr. Claude, then wiped his nose on his sleeve. "You two get going. Me and Louis will cover you," he said roughly.

Moving out at a lope, Stamper and I backtracked, looking for a place where we could slide down to the canyon floor without being seen.

"Do you have a plan, or are we just going to charge in there like the cavalry?" Stamper asked, sounding almost amused.

"I don't know. I'm thinking," I said testily. "What we need is a way to distract them for a minute. Maybe if Turley just gave them the map."

All of a sudden, I grabbed Stamper's arm, jerking him to a stop. "Hold up. I got an idea."

Without waiting, I ran back in the direction we came from. "Mr. Claude, can I borrow your coat?"

Claude eased back from the edge, peeling off his buckskin jacket. "What do you have in mind?" he asked, handing the coat to me.

"I'll show you," I said, grinning as I dropped the coat to the ground. Dropping to my knees, I jerked out his hunting knife. Stabbing the knife in the jacket, I sawed a large square out of the back of the coat. "There you go, one treasure map," I said, rolling the square piece of buckskin up. I cut a fringe off the jacket and tied it around the piece of leather.

"Why don't you go exchange this map for the young ladies?" I asked, holding the map out.

Stamper smiled, taking the piece of leather from me and rolling it in his hands. "Sounds good to me," he said.

"That won't never work," Wiesmulluer protested. "They'll never let the girls go until they look at the map to see if it's real."

"Sure, they'll want to see the map, that's what I'm counting on. When they all crowd around to look at the map, that's when we take them," I explained.

Wiesmulluer and Claude exchanged quick smiles. "What about the woman, Lilly?" Claude asked.

"As long as she doesn't try anything, leave her alone," I told them.

As we walked back, Stamper glanced at me out of the corner of his eye. "Have you got a spare gun?"

"Yeah," I replied, pulling the pistol from behind my back and showing it to him.

"Good. When you walk up to them, empty your holster and toss that gun away, but hold on to that spare. If they think you're unarmed, maybe they'll let their guard down."

Stamper's words made sense. As we closed in on their camp, Stamper took his position behind a large rock.

Gripping the phony map, I walked up to their camp, stopping in plain sight. No one noticed me as they crowded around Turley. Hetfield had his knife to the old trapper's throat, demanding the map.

"I'd say you're talking to the wrong man. I got the map," I said, a little surprised that my voice came out strong and clear.

Hands dropping to their guns, the outlaws whirled to face me. "I believe this is what you want," I said, holding up the fake map. Moving very slowly, I drew my pistol with two fingers and tossed it away from me.

Butch stepped forward, smiling greedily. Rubbing his hands together, he licked his lips. "Well now, Sheriff, it was mighty kind of you to bring it all the way out here to us. Now, hand it over."

"Not so fast," I said, holding up my hand. "I came out here to offer you a deal. I'll trade you the map for Turley and the girls."

Hetfield laughed, pointing his knife at my face. "How do we know the map is real?"

Butch looked at Turley. "How about it, old man, is it the real map?"

Turley leaned forward, squinting as he peered at the map in my hand. "Nope, might as well throw that thing in the river. It ain't the right one," Turley said easily.

I felt a pucker in my backside. That dang Turley just went and got us all killed.

Butch's hand dropped to his gun. "What are you trying to pull?" he growled.

A cold ball of fear settled in the pit of my stomach, and I knew Butch was going to kill me. I tensed myself, ready to make a wild stab at the hideout gun behind my back. I was ready to do it when I heard Hetfield chuckle.

Something about that dry laugh made my hair stand on end. I didn't have the faintest notion what Hetfield found funny, but I didn't think it meant good things for me. Butch had started to draw his pistol, but now he stopped, the weapon halfway out of the holster.

"Good try, old man, but I think we will take that map," Hetfield said, holding out his hand.

Turley swore quickly under his breath. "You dang fool, I told you that wasn't the real map."

"Shut up, old man!" Hetfield snapped, looking at me with bright, hard eyes. "Now, give me the map,"

"Let the women and Turley go first, then I'll let you have it," I said, starting to believe this just might work.

"You ain't in no position to dicker," Butch said, grinning broadly.

"Don't give it to him, Teddy. Once they have the map, they'll kill us all!" Eddy screamed.

Growling, Hetfield spun around, drawing back his hand to strike Eddy. The second I saw him start to strike Eddy, my governor blew wide open. I clean forgot about the map and the gun behind my back, as I lunged wildly at Hetfield. I collared him around the neck, jerking him back.

Out of the corner of my eye, I saw Butch pull his gun. I heard Stamper call Butch's name and heard the crash of gunfire. I expected to feel the crash of bullets tearing through me, but it never happened.

Hetfield twisted away from my grasp, clawing for his gun as he stumbled back. Without thinking, I jerked out my hideout gun and fired. The bullet slammed Hetfield back like a giant hand. Even as he fell, Hetfield struggled to raise his gun. Cocking my pistol, I fired again and kept firing until the gun was empty.

Presently I noticed the gun was empty and stopped pulling the trigger. Sucking in a deep breath to steady my frazzled nerves, I took stock.

Hetfield lay completely still, his gun thrown wide. Glancing around, I saw Stamper sitting on the ground, holding his bloody side. Crying out, Betsy rushed to his side.

A few yards away, sprawled on the ground, was the big body of Butch. The outlaw was obviously dead. He had more holes in him than a bean sieve.

Skinny lay on the ground not moving one bit. Groaning, Red crawled across the ground toward the horses. Judging by the trail of blood he was leaving, I didn't figure he'd ever make it.

"Don't anyone move," I heard Lilly shout.

Spinning around, I saw that she had Eddy around the neck with one arm, holding a gun to her side with the other.

"Now, Sheriff. If you would be so kind as to hand me the map, I'll be on my way. Anyone gets smart and the princess dies!"

I clenched my fists, the pit of my stomach churning. I heard Lilly say something, but her words floated through my head like a dream. I didn't comprehend what she said. All of my attention centered on Eddy's pale, scared face. Just seeing her like this was enough to tear my heart in two.

"Hey, redwood!" Lilly shouted, her words snapping me out of my trance. "Pick up the map and hand it to me."

Fixing a mean stare on Lilly's eyes, I tried to frighten her into giving herself up. "Are you deaf as well as dumb? I said, give me the map," Lilly repeated, punctuating her order by cocking her pistol and digging it into Eddy's side.

My eyes still locked on the two women, I bent down for the map. I felt around on the ground for the map, but finally had to drop my eyes to locate the darn thing. My hand closing over it, I straightened up.

Mr. Claude and Wiesmulluer came running up, their boots skidding on the gravel as the stopped beside me. "Give her the map," Mr. Wiesmulluer said gravely.

Nodding, I held the map out to Lilly. To take the map from my hand, Lilly had to loosen her grip on Eddy, and when she did, Eddy reacted. She stomped Lilly's foot, then slugged her on the jaw.

I guess all that fighting Eddy's been doing with me got her all practiced up, because she really clocked Lilly a good one. Fairly well dazed, Lilly staggered back a few steps, then fell flat on her fanny.

Before Lilly had a chance to recover, I jumped forward and twisted the gun from her hand. Tossing the gun away, I spun around to look at Eddy. Grabbing her by the shoulders, I looked her up and down. "Are you all right?" I asked, my voice husky.

"I'm fine," Eddy said, putting her arms around my waist. "But I sure was glad to see you coming to help."

"I hate to break up this tearful romance, but could somebody get me up," Turley bawled.

Turley had fallen backward off the rock he'd been setting on, landing on his head and neck. With his hands tied behind him, he was pretty much stuck. But he sure was fighting and frothing to get up.

Smiling to Eddy, I crossed over to the old man. I stared down at him, having half a mind to just leave him be. After all, he'd caused this whole mess. "Sufferin' stinkweed, are you gonna stand there gawking all day or help me up?" Turley bawled.

Amused, I looked over at Wiesmulluer and Claude, who were checking the outlaws to make sure they were all dead. Mr. Claude shrugged, so I helped Turley. Reaching down, I gathered him up by the front of his shirt and hauled him to his feet. Drawing my knife, I cut his hands free.

Betsy knelt beside Stamper, wringing her hands. "Is he going to be all right?" I asked.

"I don't know, he's bleeding really bad," Betsy wailed.

Betsy gladly stepped aside, letting me look at Stamper's wound. Stamper's face was gray with pain, but he was conscious.

"Aw, that doesn't look so bad. Reckon he'll live," Turley pronounced, looking over my shoulder.

Turley shook his head while Betsy helped me use Stamper's vest to make a bandage. "It's a dang wonder any of us is alive, I thought you two young pups was gonna get us all ventilated. Who's fool notion was it to bring the map, anyway? Didn't you know they'd kill us all once they had it?"

"You mean this?" Claude asked, picking up the map and unrolling it so Turley could see it.

For a minute, Turley looked stumped, then he chuckled. "Well, I'll be hornswoggled," he muttered.

"What! You mean that isn't the map?" Lilly asked, practically screaming. Grinning, Claude held the map up for her to see. Lilly's face went white and she began to cuss steadily.

"Don't worry, it fooled me too," Turley said.

As Mr. Claude and Mr. Wiesmulluer went to fetch the horses, Turley turned serious. "I reckon you boys saved my bacon, so now I'm gonna do you a favor. I'm gonna tell you where the map is. It's on a shelf under the counter at Gid's store.''

Turley laughed, pointing at the stumped looks on our faces. ''I told you I hid the map in a good place. Why, I bet ol' Gid hasn't cleaned under that counter since he opened the joint.''

By then I had Stamper ready to move, and Claude and Wiesmulluer had the horses ready. ''If you plan on carting them varmints into town, we're gonna be a couple of horses short,'' Mr. Wiesmulluer said.

''A couple of us will have to ride double. You go ahead and get Bobby into town. I'll pack these fellers in and bury them,'' I said.

''What about her?'' Claude asked, pointing to Lilly.

''Lock her in the jail. I'll have to get a hold of the U.S. marshal in Laramie to come pick her up.''

''Do you mind if I stay and ride back with you?'' Eddy asked, holding her hands behind her back and looking at the ground.

''No, I'd enjoy the company,'' I said, getting red around the ears and digging in the dirt with the toe of my boot.

Eddy stood beside me as the others loaded Stamper on his horse and started for town. As they disappeared, I started loading the dead outlaws onto their horses. Eddy was quiet as she helped tie them to their saddles. Once we had them loaded, I mounted my own horse, holding my hand down so Eddy could swing up behind me.

With the outlaws' horses stringing out behind us,

we started for town. Neither of us spoke for a long time.

"I guess you are a rich man now," Eddy commented.

"I've been thinking about that. I was thinking that maybe I could sell the map to Andrews and get my father's place back."

"Sounds nice," Eddy said softly. She circled her hands around my waist, leaning her head on my shoulder.

I touched Eddy's hand, caressing her hand with my thumb. "It could be." I turned in the saddle, looking back at her. "I was thinking, I mean, I was wondering . . . "

"What are you trying to say?"

Now, I reckon she coulda helped me, but she wasn't going to do it. Swallowing the big lump in my throat, I plunged in. "What I was wondering was, if I get my pa's ranch back, if you would like to help me run it?"

"You mean be like a hired hand?" Eddy asked, sounding mighty sweet.

"No, I meant like a wife."

Eddy let out a little squeal, squeezing me around the waist so hard, she durn near blowed my hat off my head. "I didn't think you would ever get around to asking."

We rode into town, and I dropped Eddy off at the hotel and went out to the graveyard. I'd just started digging the graves when Claude and Wiesmulluer showed up to help. Then Gid and Mr. Andrews arrived. When Turley came out to help, the affair turned into quite the party.

After we got the outlaws safely planted underground, I took their horses to the stable. I rubbed them down and fed them along with the rest of the stock.

From the stable, I crossed to the store, and as usual, the place was deserted. My knees a little slack, I circled behind the counter. Resting my hands on the counter, I took a deep breath. Ducking down, I looked under the counter.

Sure enough, sitting on the shelf and pushed to the back corner sat a piece of rolled-up leather. Snatching the leather, I pulled it out and set it on the counter. With hands that trembled a little, I unrolled it. I saw that it was indeed a map with a set of precise instructions at the bottom.

I looked at the map a long time, then made up my mind. Scooping up the map, I went to find Mr. Andrews. I found him sitting in the saloon by himself.

I walked up to his table, dropping the map in front of him. Mr. Andrews gasped, choking on his beer. "You found it," he said, picking up the map.

"That's right, and I was wondering if you would want to buy it," I said. I shot him my deal and he took it in a heartbeat.

Rubbing his hands together, Andrews licked his lips, staring at the map. "Let me get the deed and the money out of the safe," he said, his voice high and squeaky.

As Andrews swung the safe door open, his back stiffened, then he started cussing. Leaning over his shoulder, I saw a note in the safe. The note was from Bobby Stamper and it said, "I checked and your money is all here."

Andrews didn't believe the note. He went to pulling everything out of the safe. He rooted through the pile for a good five minutes, then collapsed in a chair, wiping the sweat off his brow. "It's all there," he said, grinning weakly.

His hands still shaking, he signed the deed, then counted out my money. Stuffing it in my pocket, I thanked him and tossed him the map. As I left the saloon, I heard Andrews laugh; he must've thought he got the best of me in the trade. Maybe he did, but I had what I wanted.

From the bank, I went to the jail to check on Lilly. As I entered the office, I saw the cell door standing wide open. Lunging across the office, I discovered that the cell was empty.

Swearing to myself, I spun around and ran outside. I barreled out of the office so fast that I almost ran Turley down. "What happened, boy? Did you lose another prisoner?" Turley asked, with a laugh.

"You let her out!" I exclaimed. "So she was your wife after all."

"Naw, we weren't married. She was just someone I used to see when I went to Kansas City. She went with me and pretended to be me my wife when I made out the will." For once in his life, Turley turned serious. "While they was dragging us out to that canyon, I heard her and Butch talking. Lilly and Thomas were in cahoots. They hired Butch and his men. Hetfield killed Thomas when the lawyer turned squeamish on them."

"If you knew all this, how come you let Lilly go?" I asked, scratching my head.

Turley laughed, clapping me on the back. "Shoot, boy, I need someone to see, next time I go to Kansas City. Don't worry, you won't be seeing her again. She took out of here like a house afire."

Inside, I was fuming, but I bit my tongue and kept quiet. I can't say I liked what Turley done, but I knew he probably saved everyone a lot of trouble. A trial sounded like a lot of trouble to me.

Together, we walked over to the hotel to see Stamper. Eddy and Betsy sat in chairs beside the bed as we entered the room. "Is he going to live?" I asked.

"You better believe it!" Stamper said. "We got a mine full of gold to dig up."

"Not anymore," Andrews said, barging into the room, waving the map above his head. "Teddy sold me the map. That belongs to me now!"

Now, for somebody that had been pale as a ghost, Stamper's face turned beet red in a hurry. "You did what?" he shouted, struggling to set up. "We were partners."

"He traded me the map for his father's old place and two thousand in cash, and there's nothing you can do about it."

"You had no right," Stamper started, but stopped as Turley's cackling laughter drowned out every other sound.

"You bought the map?" Turley hooted, slapping his knee and pointing at Andrews.

Andrew's face fell and he looked at the map in his hands. "You mean there's no mine?"

"Sure there was a mine, and I dug a sight of gold out of it, and I had a high time spending it," Turley said.

"Then what's so funny? Isn't this the map to the mine?"

Turley hooted, whacking Andrews across the back. "Boy, this is the best joke of all. Sure, that's the map to the mine, but there ain't no gold."

"No gold," Andrews whispered, the map slipping through his fingers.

"Nope," Turley said, beaming. "I dug out all

the gold. What you bought was an empty hole in the ground.'' He winked broadly, giving Andrews a hug. ''You don't think I would give away a mine that still had gold in it, do you?''

Andrews fell to his knees, pounding the floor with his fist. ''No gold,'' he kept mumbling over and over.

''Partner!'' Stamper shouted, holding his hand out to me. Shaking Stamper's hand, I tried to act like I knew what was going on, which I didn't.

As we filed out of the room to let Stamper rest, Eddy took my hand in hers. ''Well, at least I'm not marrying a dummy,'' she said brightly.

From Stamper's room, Eddy and I headed to the store, where Eddy was going to help me pick out a suit. Now, I didn't see the need for such things, but it was important to Eddy, so I went along.

''Can I help you, Teddy?''

I stopped short, almost fainting. Big as life, standing behind the counter all gussied up in a suit and tie, was Gid Stevens. He even had on a leather apron. ''What can I help you find?'' he asked, after Iris goosed him from behind.

''I need a suit,'' I told him.

''Back there some place,'' Gid said, pointing to the far corner of the store. ''I'll help you find one,'' he added after Iris slugged him.

''While you help the sheriff, I'll go start supper,'' Iris said, giving Gid a sweet look. On her way out, Iris shot me and Eddy a dirty look. I don't guess she was happy that I was the one that found the map.

Gid led me back to the stack of suits. Now, I reckon if it would have been just me and Gid, we'd have had a hard time finding the right suit, but Eddy helped us.

After paying Gid for the suit, Eddy and I walked outside. Turley leaned against the hitching rail. "Got you a suit, huh?" Turley asked.

"Yeah," I replied, wondering what the old coot wanted.

"You kids fixing to start ranching?"

"Yeah, Betsy and Bobby are going to be our partners."

"You know when I said you saved my life? Well, I reckon that was true, and I want to repay you." Turley pulled a piece of paper from his pocket. "This is a deed to a valley in the edge of the mountains. If you and Stamper are fixing to start a ranch, you'll need more grazing land. I'm giving this to you."

Turley grinned, handing me the deed. "You know this is the real treasure. It isn't the gold; it's the mountains themselves."

Silently agreeing with him, I took the deed. "That's very kind of you, Mr. Simmons," Eddy said, looking at the deed in my hands. "You're welcome at our house anytime."

"Why, thank you, missy. I might just take you up on that offer some day, but right now, I'm thinking of taking a trip back east. To Kansas City, maybe."

Knowing what Turley meant, I laughed, sliding my arm around Eddy's waist. We were turning away when Iris ran out of Gid's house, waving her arms over her head and screaming at the top of her lungs.

"What the . . . ," I said, making a swipe at my

pistol as a snicker escaped past Turley's lips. I glanced at Turley. "Do you know anything about that?" I growled.

Turley hooted as Iris streaked past us. "Well, not that I know anything about it, but it 'pears to me like somebody went and locked a polecat in her oven!"